Look what people are saying about Rhonda Nelson...

About *The Ex-Girlfriends' Club*...
"Uses well-developed characters in an emotional setting for a stellar story of love reunited."
—*Romantic Times BOOKreviews*

About the Men Out of Uniform miniseries...
"*The Player* (4.5), by Rhonda Nelson, is a hot, sexy story with great humor and a set-up of wonderful, strong men who it will be a joy to follow in the Men Out of Uniform series."
—*Romantic Times BOOKreviews*

"Ms. Nelson has started an amazing trilogy with the three Rangers. Humor, passion, and a little adventure set the scene for this romance, as these wonderful and somewhat damaged characters come together. Witty dialogue, along with some very touching moments, gives the feeling of realness, while these characters seek to find what they are searching for. First in the trilogy, I am already excited to see what happens to the next Ranger."
—*Coffee Time Romance*

About the Chicks in Charge miniseries...
"*Getting It Now!* (4) by Rhonda Nelson is enjoyable, with two determined, competitive characters. The sex is steamy and the setting well detailed."
—*Romantic Times BOOKreviews*

"As in the first book, the secondary characters fill out the story nicely, and there are I believe two more Chicks who need to get their men even if they don't know it yet. With exciting believable characters and hot passion Rhonda Nelson has created an exciting series, and I can't wait to see who will be getting it next."
—*A Romance Review*

Blaze™

Dear Reader,

Deep down inside, I don't think there's a woman alive who doesn't secretly adore a bad boy. There's something about a guy who flaunts natural conventions but clings to loyalty, integrity and the belief in a greater good. And when you take that kind of guy, make him a Southern gentleman and a soldier...well, he becomes pretty darned irresistible. That's Mick Chivers, the hero of this book.

A great hero like Mick deserves nothing less than a heroine who is equally wonderful. Sarah Jane Walker is kind, funny, hardworking and fierce. She's a constant champion of the underdog, one who doesn't mind taking down the people who deserve it (like her inheritance-stealing stepmother) and has a menagerie of adopted pets who call her house home. She might be tough, but she's a soft touch and she's *exactly* what Mick Chivers needs.

I've had a wonderful time with this story, and with these two characters in particular, and hope you enjoy them, as well.

For upcoming tidbits and up-to-the-minute news about my books and life in general, please check out my Web site, www.readRhondaNelson.com, and visit my group blog with Jennifer LaBrecque and Vicki Lewis Thompson at www.soapboxqueens.com. There's always a party in the castle.

Happy reading,

Rhonda

THE HELL-RAISER
Rhonda Nelson

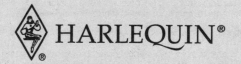

TORONTO • NEW YORK • LONDON
AMSTERDAM • PARIS • SYDNEY • HAMBURG
STOCKHOLM • ATHENS • TOKYO • MILAN • MADRID
PRAGUE • WARSAW • BUDAPEST • AUCKLAND

ISBN-13: 978-0-373-79416-4
ISBN-10:   0-373-79416-9

THE HELL-RAISER

www.eHarlequin.com

Printed in U.S.A.

ABOUT THE AUTHOR

A Waldenbooks bestselling author, two-time RITA®
Award nominee and *Romantic Times BOOKreviews*
Reviewers' Choice nominee, Rhonda Nelson writes
hot romantic comedy for Harlequin Blaze. In
addition to a writing career she has a husband, two
adorable kids, a black Lab and a beautiful bichon
frise who dogs her every step. She and her family
make their chaotic but happy home in a small town
in northern Alabama.

Books by Rhonda Nelson

HARLEQUIN BLAZE
75—JUST TOYING AROUND
81—SHOW & TELL
115—PICTURE ME SEXY
140—THE SEX DIET
158—1-900-LOVER
172—GETTING IT GOOD!
217—GETTING IT RIGHT!
223—GETTING IT NOW!
255—THE PLAYER
277—THE SPECIALIST
283—THE MAVERICK
322—THE EX-GIRLFRIENDS'
     CLUB
361—FEELING THE HEAT
400—THE LONER

**HARLEQUIN
TEMPTATION**
973—UNFORGETTABLE
1007—GETTING IT!

**HARLEQUIN
SIGNATURE SELECT**
THE FUTURE WIDOWS' CLUB
THREE GUYS YOU'LL
   NEVER DATE
"Her Hero?"

To Beverly Barton, for taking the time to introduce a writer-wannabe to Heart of Dixie, RWA, and whose single act of kindness and generosity unwittingly changed my life forever. I am so very thankful for your unfailing support, guidance and friendship.

1

NICE ASS, Mick Chivers thought, staring at one of the multiple pictures he'd been given of his target. His reaction was hardly appropriate given the circumstances—first assignment, new job at Ranger Security, chance to start over, yada yada yada—but he'd never given a second thought to propriety before and wasn't about to start now. He absently rubbed his temple and slouched lower in his chair, seemingly unconcerned, confident and unaware of the four pairs of eyes currently trained on him. He smothered a snort.

As if.

But Sarah Jane Walker *did* have a nice ass. Even in this out-of-focus sorry excuse for a photograph. Who'd taken it? he wondered, irritated. A monkey? Granted, Mick was only a hobby photographer, but he knew his way around a camera well enough to do better. His moody gaze slid back to her face. She had a nice mouth, too. And that hair. Long, thick and wavy, falling well below the back of her bra, a pretty dark blond with caramel highlights. He almost smiled.

And he had to admit, the tool belt was a nice touch.

"An architectural salvage expert, eh?" he asked no one in particular. "What exactly is it that she does?"

Though he didn't look up, Mick could feel Brian Payne's intense blue gaze. Good construction prevented the noisy downtown Atlanta sounds from seeping into the room, but Mick imagined he heard the occasional honk of a horn.

The other three men in the lounge area of their office had taken chairs around a big coffee table laden with a variety of snacks. Jamie Flanagan nursed a high-energy drink. Guy McCann idly flipped through a sports magazine. Hands dangling between his knees, Lucas "Huck" Finn—Mick's good friend, former unit mate and no small reason he'd been offered this job after his hasty exit from the military—leaned forward and studied him closely, those keen gray eyes probing for answers Mick was disinclined to give.

What was there to say, really, other than he'd screwed up and nearly cost another soldier his life?

It was Payne who finally answered. "In a nutshell, she goes into old houses—usually ones that are slated for demolition—and saves everything of value. Mantels, crown molding, built-ins, stained glass, doors. Those sorts of things." He leaned against the back of Flanagan's chair. "Interesting work for a woman, but our research says she's very good at what she does. Her father was in the construction business. Apparently, she apprenticed under him."

So she learned her trade from her father, Mick thought. How novel. The only thing he'd ever learned from his old man was how to leave. His mother, too, for that matter. He'd certainly gotten used to watching their taillights disappear every time they dropped him off at Mars Hill Academy, a rigorous old military school located in the beautiful hills of North Carolina. Far enough from their eastern Kentucky home to put distance between them, but drivable in the event of an emergency. Or so he'd overheard his mother say once to a friend.

Deemed "a problem child" at an early age, Mick had been shipped off to military school after the sixth grade—it probably would have been sooner if his parents could have found a facility to accept him—and had only been allowed home over the Christmas holidays and summer break.

And since he'd spent the latter with his paternal grandfather, Charlie—usually repairing the barn or building a new addition onto the old house—instead of his parents, Mick could honestly say that he'd typically spent two weeks out of the year at what other people actually called "home." He inwardly shuddered at those awkward holiday memories. The forced smiles, the fake happiness, when it was all too plain they couldn't wait to send him back, to be rid of him, as though his being born and screwing up their lives had been *his* fault. Mick passed a hand over his face and swallowed the bitter taste in his mouth.

It was no damned wonder he hated Christmas.

Water under the bridge, he told himself, releasing a shallow breath. Hell, they'd actually done him a favor. Despite the somewhat harsh and überstructured format—and the occasional thrashing for mischief— he'd thrived at military school. He'd learned to love his country, to revere the men who'd founded it and, more importantly, to honor the soldiers who'd died for it by becoming a U.S. Army Ranger and taking up their cause. He'd learned that honor was rewarded, deceit punished, that hard work tested the measure of a man and boundaries were meant to be pushed. Another half smile flirted with his lips. Actually, if you asked any of his former instructors, they'd probably say he'd learned that lesson best of all. He hadn't been nicknamed The Hell-raiser for nothing.

One of these days you're going to go too far, Chivers.

Regret and disgrace formed an enormous ball in his gut. The one-of-these-days warning had come true recently, much to his shame and horror, and was the main reason he'd left the military. A vision of Carson Wells's agonized face rose in Mick's mind's eye, tormenting him with an image he'd never forget. If that bullet had been an inch higher and to the left, it would've surely killed him. Too close, Mick thought, because as predicted, *he'd* gone too far.

He'd made the call and the mistake.

Never again.

Fortunately—or at least that's what he was telling himself—Colonel Carl Garrett had referred him to Ranger Security. Landing a job with the elite agency of former Rangers—men from his background—was a coup, one he was certain he would celebrate when he was less inclined to hate himself. At the moment, it was all he could do to sit here and pretend he wasn't losing his mind right along with his life and career. That he wasn't the eternal screwup his father had always claimed.

Furthermore, he honestly didn't have any idea why

they'd hired him. He'd made a monumental error. He'd almost cost another soldier his life because of his reckless judgment. How could they possibly think he deserved this job? Could he do it? Certainly. But he imagined the only reason he'd scored the hire was because Huck had gone to bat for him. And at the moment, that little bit of knowledge was the only thing that would ensure that he did a good job.

He'd be damned before he let another friend down.

Speaking of friends, he should really call Levi, Mick thought, ashamed that he'd avoided contact with his unit mate. Mick had met both Lucas Finn and Levi McPherson during Jump School. Somewhere between the grueling training and commiserating beers, the three had become especially close friends. Having been in an all-guy environment for most of his life, one that by its very nature fostered a unique blend of competition and camaraderie, Mick had made some great buddies over the years. But the dynamic among the three of them had always been more like that of brothers.

Other than his grandfather, they were the closest thing to a family he'd ever had.

When things had gone south recently, it was Huck who'd helped him find a job, but Levi had had his back, as well. He'd actually been a member of the team on that ill-fated mission, and Mick was having a harder time facing him. Hell, even talking to him. Levi had personally witnessed his mistake, and knowing that made it too damned hard for Mick to look him in the eye. In short, he was ashamed, and until he figured out how to cope with the screwup, he was better off avoiding his friend. Cowardly? No doubt. But necessary to his questionable sanity at the moment.

Rather than linger on things he couldn't change, Mick exhaled a short sigh and mentally reviewed the mess of his first case. And it was a convoluted quagmire of personal crap he'd just as soon stay out of. Unfortunately, staying out of it wasn't in his new job description.

"So let me get this straight. We've been hired by Chastity Walker—"

"Sarah Jane's stepmother," McCann interjected.

"Who is also Sarah Jane's age and most hated enemy," Flanagan added with a wry look.

"—to catch Sarah Jane trying to steal some of her deceased father's possessions."

"Possessions that Sarah Jane claims are part of her inheritance," Payne added.

Mick frowned. "There's no will?"

Payne shrugged. "Not according to Chastity, and with the absence of a will, everything goes to the next of kin. As the wife, that's her."

"What about according to Sarah Jane?" Mick asked, smelling a rat. Something about this didn't feel right. Why would Chastity go to the trouble of hiring their services for something so small? So petty? He knew women could be like that, of course, and it certainly didn't seem like there was any love lost between these two, but… He was picking up a weird vibe on this one.

"Sarah Jane insists there was a will, but neither Chastity nor the attorney who supposedly drafted it has produced it." Payne grimaced. "Like I said, I'm not sure about this one, and we won't be a party to anything illegal. Right now, we have the facts according to our client. If she's lying, then naturally that will change things, and you can respond however you see fit." He paused. "As it stands, we know that Sarah Jane, in particular, is after a pipe that belonged to her father, and her mother's antique wedding dress." Payne shrugged, looking uncomfortably skeptical. "Chastity will not give up the pipe and insists that she donated the dress to a local historical society after it had been part of an exhibit."

Mick shot him a questioning glance. "And you believe her?"

"Not particularly. Right now though, operating on what we know from our client, our job is to keep an eye on Sarah Jane. If she does anything illegal, document the evidence and turn it over to Chastity so that she can do with it what she will."

Flanagan snorted. "Hell, Payne, she's already had Sarah Jane arrested once for assault and battery. You know what she's going to do with it."

Mick felt his lips twitch, and he flipped to the back of the file, where Sarah Jane's mutinous mug shot stared up at him. She had wide, compelling, pale brown eyes—the shade of his favorite toffee candy, Mick thought—which were ringed in a darker hue, making them all the more interesting. A single green leaf had gotten tangled up in those long tresses and a smudge of dirt shadowed one rather plump cheek. Her chin was tilted up in a defiant little angle, seemingly daring the person behind the camera to say a word. The fight might have been broken up, but it hadn't yet left her—every line of her body seemed tensed and ready for action. Mick recognized that look, that particular brand of energy. God knows he'd felt it often enough, more so than was prudent. It was no small part of the reason his nickname had actually fit.

It was also the reason one hell-raiser typically recognized another. And Sarah Jane Walker looked like she didn't need a stick to stir shit with the best of them. Unbelievably, a current of heat snaked through Mick's groin, and his palms tingled, itching to wipe that curiously sexy bit of dirt from her cheek. Slip the pad of his thumb over that ripe bottom lip.

Aw, hell. This can't be good.

McCann chuckled. "According to the police report I read, Sarah Jane mopped the deck with her," he said. "It's no wonder Chastity is out for blood."

"From the looks of things, the woman has got her home and her inheritance. Shouldn't that be enough?" Mick asked, secretly pleased that Sarah Jane had gotten the better of his temporary employer. Why? Who knew? Because she was hot? Possibly. Because it sounded as if Sarah Jane was the underdog here? That, too. Not that he should care, because it wasn't his problem and he had enough of his own to deal with. Still, he'd always been a sucker for both, and when he factored in the tool belt and hellcat attitude… Well, he couldn't deny it made her all the more appealing.

He had a sneaking suspicion he wasn't supposed to find his target appealing. Some of that keen Ranger training rearing its head, Mick thought, stifling the ridiculous urge to laugh.

"I know that it's a bit dodgy," Payne admitted. "This isn't a typical kind of case for us, so use discretion, Mick. If, in your observations, you discover that your mission conflicts with justice, then act accordingly."

Mick nodded, then looked down at the folder in his hand, flipping back to the front page. Where was he headed again? Monarch Grove, Georgia. Population 2,478. He smothered another laugh. It was a damned good thing they'd developed a decent cover for him, because blending into a town that small sure as hell wouldn't be easy.

"So I'm with *Designing Weekly,* an architectural magazine based out of Atlanta?"

"Right. You're the photographer and you've been sent ahead to shoot the spread." Flanagan slid several issues as well as a couple of books on architecture across the coffee table. "You're new, which explains your lack of bylines or photo credits. We've contacted her and set everything up. You'll be able to follow her around without any problem, which will enable you to learn her routine." He shrugged. "Naturally, we expect her to make her move at night, provided she's going to. So you'll want to pay particular attention to her then."

"There aren't any motels in Monarch Grove, so we've booked you into a B and B near the town square," Payne added. "Luckily, it's only a couple of blocks from Sarah Jane's place and it seems to be the morning hot spot for breakfast."

Mick felt a sardonic smile slide over his lips. "It sounds very Norman Rockwell."

"And just think," McCann said, grinning broadly. "You'll be there during the Fried Pie Festival."

Flanagan sighed contentedly. "Apple is a personal favorite of mine. Be sure and bring back a few, would you?"

Mick stared. It took a moment for him to realize

Flanagan was serious. "Sure," he said, for lack of anything better.

"You've got two weeks," Payne told him, bringing a brisk end to the briefing. "Call if you run into any trouble."

And just like that, Mick was dismissed. No "do you think you can handle it?" No second-guessing him. No peering over his shoulder despite the major screwup he'd recently committed.

Just genuine trust in his abilities.

He knew a single second of joy before the inevitable dread settled over his shoulders. He sure as hell hoped their confidence wasn't misplaced.

Particularly Huck's.

TROUBLED, HUCK WATCHED his friend gather the file and paraphernalia for his new mission and, trademark confidence in place, calmly walk from the room.

Payne paused a moment, then looked at Huck and quirked a brow. "Garrett recommended him and Levi McPherson made a personal appeal on his behalf for this job. But you've worked with him. What's your read?"

"He's hurting," Huck said, unsurprised that Levi, too, had spoken up for their friend. "His confidence is shot. He's ashamed of his mistake, of what it could have potentially cost another soldier." He shook his head, wishing he could do something to rattle his old unit mate back into action. Huck had thought the Ranger Security position would make Mick realize that he was still worthy, that while he was no longer a Ranger in Uncle Sam's Army, he could still use those skills. Still share the mentality and camaraderie with men from his background. It had certainly done wonders for Huck after his accident.

McCann's usually jovial gaze turned serious. "We've all been there and survived the worst."

Danny Levison's death, Huck knew. The group had shared their story with him shortly after he'd come on board. Danny had been more than their unit mate, he'd been one of their best friends. And each one of them, in some way, had felt responsible for his death.

Flanagan swallowed. "Mick'll come around," he said. "It's just going to take a little time."

Payne's cool blue eyes found Huck's. "Is he up to this? I'm not asking if he's capable—I know that, otherwise we wouldn't have hired him. But is he emotionally ready for work?"

Though he admittedly had his doubts when it came to his friend's state of mind, Huck merely smiled and said the one thing he knew they'd all understand. "He's a soldier, Payne. He'll be fine."

Frankly, if you asked Huck, getting his daredevil, hell-raising friend right back into the action was the best possible treatment for what ailed him. His lips quirked. And sending him to Podunk, Georgia, to tail a hot little she-devil sounded even better. Sarah Jane Walker certainly looked like she'd give Mick a run for his money.

And knowing his friend, the chase would be just what the doctor ordered.

2

"SLIMY BASTARD," Sarah Jane Walker muttered under her breath as she exited the attorney's office. She should have known that as long as Chastity was balling her late father's legal counsel, Sarah Jane wasn't going to get anything out of him. She inwardly snorted. Like most men who came into close proximity with Chastity's enormous breasts, Cecil Simmons was thinking with a part of his anatomy that didn't house a brain. She grimaced.

And she'd begun to think the part on his shoulders didn't have much of a brain, either.

Having spotted her, Mason Webster, her devoted assistant, straightened away from her aging work truck. "Well?" he asked. "How did it go?"

With an exasperated huff and a few irritated epithets, Sarah Jane opened the door and slid behind the wheel. She grabbed a ponytail holder from the gearshift—one of many—and pulled her hair up. *Ahh. Much better.* Damn this August heat. Fall wouldn't make an appearance until late October, and this was the time of year she began to really long for it.

"The same way it went last time and the time before that. Horribly." She cranked the ignition, then backed away from the curb and headed toward the Milton Plantation, another old beauty sadly destined for demolition. Sure, the floor was falling in and it was a structural nightmare, but the place was still worth saving. Or at least it was to her. Unfortunately, she couldn't afford to keep it from being torn down, but if she could save a few pieces—a mantel here, a door there, a bit of molding—then she'd at least feel a little better about it. All of its history wouldn't be lost.

"He still can't find the will?" Mason said, outrage lining his peach-fuzzed, freckled face. The boy was determined to grow a beard, though why he'd ever want one was a mystery to Sarah Jane. Particularly in this heat, she thought, turning the air-conditioning up another notch. "You know he's lying, don't you?" Mason continued. "I don't know why you won't let me help you. I could beat the whereabouts of your father's will out of him, I know I could." His fuzzy chin jutted out belligerently.

Sarah Jane stifled the grin that immediately rose to her lips. Frankly, she thought she had a better chance of taking on Cecil Simmons in a fight than Mason did. Her gaze slid to her one and only employee.

Short, thick through the middle, with scrawny arms and even scrawnier legs, plus thin and wispy strawberry-blond hair, Mason put her in mind of a poorly proportioned scarecrow. It was really a pity that a person's outside didn't always match was what inside because, if that were the case, Mason would be a brilliant hottie with a loyal heart. She inwardly smiled. He was certainly devoted to her, and she could thank a single act of kindness and her hot temper for that.

Being different anywhere was difficult, but being different in a little town like Monarch Grove, Georgia, really took courage. Unlike most of the kids his age, Mason wasn't into sports, pop culture and trendy music. At nineteen, he was a Trekkie with an ear for jazz, and preferred reading sci-fi novels to playing video games.

On the night she'd come to his rescue, he'd been showing his newest eBay find, a vintage Borg talking head lunch box, to a couple of equally unique friends at Mabel's Diner, when a group of so-called cool kids snatched the lunch box out of Mason's hands and proceeded to play keep-away with it. Sarah Jane had stepped in, reclaimed the object, then roundly reamed out the pranksters.

Mason had shown up at her workshop behind her house the next day and he'd been with her ever since. He'd redesigned her Web site, installed better business software and updated her computer, organized her office and her time and generally kept her on task. She didn't know what she'd do once he finished college and moved on, but she supposed she'd just have to cross that bridge when she came to it. But she couldn't let him fight her battles for her.

Besides, if she was going to drag anyone into this mess, it would be her long-time best friend, Tina Martinese. The two of them had been buddies since birth. Born a couple of days apart to families who were very close, she and Tina had literally grown up together. Tina's parents had recently bought an RV and were touring the country, one national park at a time. Though she wasn't a sister by blood, Tina was definitely the sister of Sarah Jane's heart.

Petite and curvy, with dark hair and pretty hazel eyes, Tina was fearless, fierce and funny, and could cook like nobody's business. She was also carrying a torch for one of their local boys in blue, Chase Collins. Unfortunately, Chase's fear of commitment was almost as legendary as Tina's lasagna. Speaking of which, Sarah Jane would be enjoying that particular delicacy this evening. But she couldn't think about that right now.

She had a more pressing matter to attend to.

Like getting her inheritance back from her money-grubbing slut of a stepmother—Chastity Pigg…Walker. Sarah Jane grimaced with distaste. It still killed her that she shared the same last name with her most hated enemy, one who, gallingly, was her own age. Wasn't it bad enough that she'd unwittingly shared a high-school boyfriend and later, her own father, with her nemesis?

For reasons Sarah Jane had never been able to comprehend, Chastity had always had it in for her. In grade school, she'd tormented Sarah Jane about her fat cheeks, her affinity for dirt—she'd never minded if her pants had grass stains—and her penchant for playing tag with the boys as opposed to primping on the playground with the girls.

In high school, Chastity had taken a different tack—she'd made it a point to steal any boy Sarah Jane had ever liked. In most cases, it had been more annoying than hurtful, but senior year, when Chastity had made a move on Luke Anderson—her first *real* love—and Luke had succumbed, that had stung. Sarah Jane had written him off, of course, because if Luke hadn't had the brains and wherewithal to stay out of the back of his truck with a sleazy tramp like Chastity, then he sure as hell didn't deserve *her.* And he was an idiot, to boot.

Turned out her father had been an idiot, as well.

An image of his dear face rose in her mind's eye and a hard lump formed in her throat. God, how she missed him. Missed both of her parents, but the unexpected death of her father had hit her harder. For years after her mom had died—damned breast cancer—George, better known as "Tough" Walker, had remained single. He'd insisted that her mother had been the only woman for him. They'd been well matched, had shared the same interests and were utterly devoted to one another.

To say that Sarah Jane went into shock when her father had started dating Chastity would be an understatement of epic proportions.

Though she'd voiced a bit of displeasure, Sarah Jane had eventually bitten her tongue and opted to give her father the benefit of the doubt, remembering years of sound decisions and good judgment, of bear hugs and pancake breakfasts. She'd been certain that he'd come to his senses, realize Chastity was a soul-sucking, brainless, manipulative bitch with questionable morals and, in short order, cut her loose.

Instead, to her shock, shame, embarrassment and horror, he'd done the unthinkable—he'd married her.

And while Sarah Jane hated Chastity with every fiber of her being, she'd loved her father more. He'd seemed happier than he'd been in years and, though she was relatively certain she could have put a stop to it, how selfish could she be? Her dad had assured her that the house—the one that she, her mother and father had painstakingly restored—would still be hers to do with what she wished. She could live in it herself, or sell it and take the proceeds to buy another. He'd also promised her she'd get a few other items he knew her mother would have wanted her to have.

Frankly, the idea of Chastity living in the very house that her parents had shared made Sarah Jane's flesh crawl. But the idea that the woman was actually trying to keep it…that set her blood on fire.

She'd *seen* her father's will. She *knew* what she was supposed to inherit—in addition to the house, there'd been a sizable savings account, part of which had been proceeds from her mother's estate.

The first month or so after the funeral, Sarah Jane had been too grief stricken to press Chastity about the will. Though she'd hated her—she had gotten the impression that the woman had genuinely cared for her father— Sarah Jane hadn't wanted to be cruel. Kicking her butt to the curb had seemed particularly harsh. But when one month turned to four and her dear stepmother decided to buy a new Hummer, then had gotten a tummy tuck, Sarah Jane decided that the time for being nice was over.

She'd asked for her father's pipe. Chastity had told her it was simply too dear and she just couldn't bring herself to part with it.

She'd asked for her mother's wedding dress—which had originally belonged to her grandmother. Chastity said she'd cleaned out the attic and was certain the gown had gone into the trash. It hadn't, Sarah Jane learned later, when she'd seen it on display at a local historical fair. At that point, she'd decided that merely *asking* for things wasn't going to work—it was time to *take* them.

And that's when she'd discovered her father's will had vanished. He'd always kept important papers in the filing cabinet in his study, but when she looked, the entire file was gone. And not only had the document vanished from the house, it had disappeared from the attorney's office, as well. Coincidence?

She thought not.

Sarah Jane had accepted that, in all likelihood, Chastity had done away with the copy locked in her father's filing cabinet in his study. But she was holding out hope that Cecil had sense enough not to destroy the original. She suspected he'd locate the will when he and Chastity finished their "business," but she didn't have any idea how long that was going to take. And meanwhile, Chastity was running through her inheritance as if it were water.

Since beating the hell out of her stepmother—an altercation that had occurred shortly after Sarah Jane discovered her mother's wedding gown at the annual historical fair—hadn't produced the desired results, she had decided it was time to take a different tack.

She was going to steal them.

Actually, *steal* wasn't exactly the right word. Stealing implied that the stuff had never been hers to start with, but that wasn't the case. Sarah Jane liked the word *rescue* better. She was going to rescue her things—via a little breaking and entering, because her stepmonster had changed the locks. Then she planned on slipping into Cecil's office and doing a thorough search for her father's so-called misplaced will. She felt a determined smile slide over her lips.

Clearly the lawyer hadn't looked hard enough.

Frustrated, Sarah Jane aimed the truck down the long gravel drive. The Milton Plantation rose up like a tired but beautiful old belle. It was a shame there was no way to save it.

"Looks like he's here already," Mason remarked.

"Who? Oh," Sarah Jane said, spying an olive-green SUV parked near the side of the old house. "The *Designing Weekly* guy." A flush of pleasure washed through her. Talk about a bright spot in an otherwise dismal last few months.

Sarah Jane had always been a fan of the magazine. A regular subscriber, she pored over her copy every week, appreciating the articles pertaining to restoration, specifically. The fact that the editors wanted to do a feature on her and her business was a particular coup. Granted, she had a pretty sizable clientele in the greater Atlanta area, but *Designing Weekly* had distribution all over the United States. She and Mason fully expected business to boom after the article ran—they'd been getting the Web site and inventory ready in preparation for the event.

The presumed windfall couldn't come at a better time. Business was good—she wasn't behind on her bills or anything like that—but her truck had more than 200,000 miles on the engine, her tools were showing wear and she didn't expect her air-conditioning unit to make it though this abysmal, wretched, miserable summer. In short, she had a lot of big expenses looming. Knowing the money would soon be there to cover them took an enormous weight off her shoulders.

Furthermore, money aside, restoration was her passion. Anything that furthered her cause, made home builders more aware of other options and saved bits and pieces of brilliant architecture was a coup.

Sarah Jane pulled up alongside the SUV, waved and smiled at the man seated behind the wheel. Due to the tinted glass, she couldn't get a good look at him. "What's his name again?" she asked Mason from the side of her mouth, thankful he stayed on top of things like that.

"Mick Chivers. He's a photographer and he'll be in town for the next two weeks. Through next Friday."

She knew that. At first, she'd thought it was a bit odd for the magazine to send a photographer out to follow her around for two weeks, without the actual writer, who'd arrive a few weeks later. But since she wasn't in the magazine business, this could be the norm for all she knew. Actually, it would work out quite well. It would take her approximately two weeks to finish the job, salvaging everything she could find from this old house. He could see the project through from start to finish and document it, frame by frame, for the piece.

"He's staying at Clara's," Mason said, gathering his Star Trek thermos, snack bag and MP3 player.

Sarah Jane chuckled and collected her gear, as well. "Where else is there to stay in Monarch Grove?"

The lone B and B was the only game in town for occasional travelers, and did most of its business during the upcoming Fried Pie Festival. Thanks to Tina, it was also the best place to have breakfast. Or any other meal for that matter, in Sarah Jane's opinion, though Mabel's Diner was a close second.

Naturally, she would never say that in Clara's presence—there was a certain rivalry between the two older women. Mabel and Clara were both members of the Monarch Grove Community Theater and were constantly vying for the same parts. When Mabel took the lead roll as the Unsinkable Molly Brown in the last production, Clara had actually put on black, mourning the part. Since then, the food war, which had been intense to start with, had increasingly escalated. If Clara was serving chocolate pie for dessert, then Mabel would invariably offer chocolate chocolate pie. The only people who seemed to benefit were the actual patrons, because the food was always fabulous.

"Think we ought to warn him?" Mason asked.

Sarah Jane grinned. "About what? Clara's ever-changing hair color, her penchant for show tunes or Byron?"

"All of the above," Mason said, affecting a shudder. "But particularly Byron. Mick's a guy, Sarah Jane. Someone should say something."

"Nah. He'll find out soon enough on his own." Sarah Jane felt her lips twitch. No doubt Mick Chivers would be hearing Clara's warbly, off-pitch rendition of "Give My Regards to Broadway" this evening. The poor man. As for Byron, the B and B's resident ghost, how exactly did one warn a person about a homosexual spook?

Pasting a smile onto her face, she opened the door and stepped out of her truck. The hot August sun beat down on her head, the humid air instantly bathed her skin in sticky heat and, though she wore a pair of pricey sunglasses, she found herself squinting. Dimly she heard the click of another door, the resounding *ding-ding-ding* issuing from his SUV. She heard the crunch of gravel beneath a booted foot, then he emerged from behind the open door, and suddenly that persistent dinging took on another meaning completely.

Her breath—what little of it the stifling temperature hadn't robbed from her lungs—caught in her throat. A single strip of gooseflesh raced down her spine, then up again and settled at the back of her neck, making her scalp tingle. Her palms dampened, her mouth went dry and a buzz of sexual adrenaline ran through her body, igniting her nipples, and concentrated in a tornado of swirling sensation directly below her naval.

Sarah Jane was twenty-eight years old, had been sexually active for eight of those years and had never— *never*—set eyes on a man and literally quivered so hard she felt her insides vibrate.

Unaccustomed to not being completely in control of her reactions, she told herself that her quickie breakfast didn't agree with her, that she was probably getting sick.

Yeah, that *had* to be it. Really.

Furthermore, Mick Chivers didn't look like any photographer she'd ever seen—he seemed too big, too vibrant for such a patient occupation. Though he was roughly a car length from where her feet were rooted to the driveway, and he hadn't so much as moved once he'd seen her, she could feel the restlessness, the sheer energy, rolling off of him in waves. She could sense it in every line of his six-and-a-half-foot-plus, magnificently proportioned body. She even fancied she could see it swirling around him.

Danger, wickedness, irreverence.

Instinct told her that if she played chicken with this guy, she'd definitely lose. The devil in her instantly recognized the devil in him, and the knowledge equally terrified and thrilled her. He had that fearlessness, that reckless edge that was both compelling and sexy. He put her in mind of a wild mustang—proud and untamable, but beautiful and...lonely? she thought, struck with the curious but unmistakable temptation to comfort him. From what?

Who knew? But she couldn't deny the feeling, the intrinsic knowledge that this guy was an island unto himself.

And at the moment, he liked it that way.

A cool khaki linen shirt stretched over a pair of mouthwateringly wide shoulders, and the short sleeves revealed arms that were muscled and well honed. He might spend a little time in the gym, but for whatever reason, Sarah Jane got the impression that hard work had put the majority of those muscles into place rather than a daily exercise regimen.

Brown hair the shade of melting chocolate lay in messy, irreverent waves on top of his head, and a jaw, chiseled as though straight from the hand of Michelangelo, rounded out a face that was too masculine to be called pretty, but was gorgeous all the same. Wide, firm, full lips casually drifted into a smile, one that held just the slightest hint of wicked arrogance, causing a deep dimple to emerge in the smooth hollow of his right cheek. A tremble eddied through Sarah Jane's midsection and she longed to see his eyes, which, like hers, were hidden behind a pair of dark shades.

He strode around the hood of his car, camera bag over his shoulder, and extended his hand. Huge, callused, with blunt-tipped fingers and masculine veins. In a word, wonderful. Strong. Sensual. You could tell a lot about people by their hands, Sarah Jane thought dimly, as she slipped her palm against his. Another little shock of sensation bolted through her and she smiled, deciding to pretend it didn't happen. What the hell? It had worked for Scarlett O'Hara, hadn't it?

"Mick Chivers," he said, his voice a raspy baritone that sizzled along her nerve endings and induced the irrational urge to weep. Or worse, giggle. Was it too much to hope that he'd sound like Mickey Mouse sucking helium?

Evidently.

No! No! No! Not him! Not now! She didn't have time for sex, much less an inconvenient sexual attraction.

"I'm Sarah Jane Walker," she finally managed to say, her own voice a thready whisper she barely recognized. From the corner of her eye, she saw Mason's amiable face take on an odd look. No doubt he was wondering what the hell had happened to his employer. "It's, er…a pleasure to meet you."

She'd never thought about those particular words before, but the mundane greeting suddenly took on a whole new meaning. She resisted the urge to jerk her hand back and bite her fist. In this case, pleasure and torture took on a synonymous translation—she could honestly say the pleasure of being near him was torturing her.

Furthermore, those lips of his looked even better up close. His top one, in particular, was rather overfull, and when he smiled, a bit off center. There was something equally sexy and endearing about that little imperfection.

And he was going to be with her for the next two weeks. Second beyond second, minute by minute, hour after hour. She felt a trickle of sweat slide between her breasts and, because she'd somehow managed to lose her mind in the past minute, imagined it was his tongue. Jeez, God, and she'd thought it was hot before.

3

THE FUZZY, OUT-OF-FOCUS pictures and the mug shot hadn't done this woman justice, Mick thought as he stared down into Sarah Jane's intriguing face. And the small, but curiously firm, hand presently shaking his had an even more interesting effect on the rest of his body—it immediately went into a full-throttle burn that had nothing to do with the blazing temperatures.

This was internal.

Not good, he noted, once again using those keen Ranger skills to deduce the obvious. A stream of blistering epithets raced through his mind, thanks to the environment and the unfortunate instant attraction currently blowing the top off his personal thermometer.

She was his target, for chrissakes. Off-limits. Out of bounds.

Naturally, that made her all the more appealing to him.

"Welcome to Monarch Grove," Sarah Jane murmured. She had a nice voice, Mick decided. The perfect combination of throaty and feminine, and he instinctively knew she'd have a great laugh. Anyone who smiled so openly certainly wouldn't try to repress a hearty chuckle. She was refreshing, he decided. The women he occasionally dated—and that was a very loose term, because his career hadn't left much time for traditional dating—tended to have more...affected charms.

There was absolutely nothing affected about the woman standing in front of him.

If she wore any makeup at all, she'd applied it with a very light hand. Dressed in a pale pink T-shirt screen-printed with her operation's name, Reclaiming the Past, an Architectural Salvage Company, and a pair of white denim shorts, her thick caramel-streaked hair pulled into a ponytail, Sarah Jane simultaneously epitomized sexy, fresh-scrubbed and ready to work. Impressed, he stared down into her smiling face and wished he could see her eyes.

The sunglasses, he decided moodily, were an attractive nuisance.

"No trouble finding the place, I see," another voice interjected.

Mick reluctantly tore his gaze away from Sarah Jane and directed his attention to the young man standing beside her.

Ah, her protector, he thought, noting the territorial stance the young guy had taken next to his employer. Mick would have expected Sarah's second in command to be both older and a bit more physically capable of actually *helping* her. Not to say this guy couldn't...but he didn't look like he did a whole lot of heavy lifting.

"Not at all," he replied casily. "You must be Mason. Great directions."

Seeming to relax a bit, Mason smiled. "When did you get into town?"

"Just now, actually," Mick told him. "I thought I'd check into the bed-and-breakfast later this afternoon, after we finish up for the day."

"You've already made reservations though, right?" Sarah Jane asked, a furrow of concern emerging between her delicate brows. He was suddenly hit with the almost irrepressible urge to trace that gentle slope with his tongue.

"Before I left Atlanta, yes," he said, struggling to focus. He hadn't personally booked the room, of course; Payne had taken care of that. So Mick knew he had a place to stay.

"Oh, good," she said, seemingly relieved. "Ordinarily there's always a room available at Clara's, but during the Fried Pie Festival space is at a premium."

He grinned. Ah, yes. The annual Fried Pie Festival. Monarch Grove's dubious claim to fame. "I saw the banners," he said. *All five thousand of them,* he added silently.

As though she was reading his mind, a wry smile tugged at the corner of her distractingly ripe mouth. "You know us Southerners. We take our pie seriously."

"And if it's fried, all the better," Mason added. He nodded toward his boss and grinned, rocking back on his heels. "Sarah Jane has taken the grand prize with her blackberry fried pies for the past three years. She's the one to beat."

Impressed, Mick darted his gaze back to her once more. "Blackberry, eh?" The fruit suited her, he decided. Protected by thorny branches, but the reward was tart and sweet. He imagined her savoring a big juicy berry, and felt his dick twitch in his jeans. *Damn.* "I'll have to be sure and try one."

"I'm sure you'll get your fill of pie while you're here," she said dryly, then released a breath and glanced toward the house. "I suppose we should get started." She hesitated, shooting Mick a look of uncertainty. "I'm, uh…not exactly sure how this is supposed to work. Did you want to get any pictures of us, or of the house as it stands, before we get started? Or are you just going to snap photos as we work? This is all quite new to me."

To Mick, too, but now that she mentioned it, he supposed he would need to take several photos of her individually for the supposed "spread." A perk, he decided, wishing he'd been acting more like a professional photographer instead of standing here gawking at her. Losing focus two minutes into his first assignment for Ranger Security sure as hell wasn't good. The memory of Huck's concerned gaze rose like Lazarus from the dead in his mind's eye, making his face heat with shame.

Mick withdrew his camera from the bag and adjusted a couple of settings. "Actually, it would be great if I could get a few shots of you now."

Sarah Jane nodded. "Sure. Where do you want us?"

Mick paused to peruse the grounds, and for the first time, really looked at the old house and surrounding area. The Milton Plantation was a sad old belle who, past her prime and beyond usefulness, appeared to have been abandoned by her owners. The lawn had long ago surrendered the fight to creeping crabgrass and tall weeds. Ragweed and Queen Anne's lace, their noble heads bobbing in the slight breeze, dotted the neglected landscape. A half-dozen live oaks, Spanish moss dripping from their limbs, provided shade beneath their leafy, gnarled branches. A single rosebush, decked out in dozens of fist-size, pale pink blooms, defiantly clung to the side of the house near the corner of the porch and curled around the rotten, gap-toothed railing.

Fancy fretwork sagged like spent, dirty lace from the eaves of the enormous two-story structure, and pretty spindles—the few that remained around the upper porch—listed slightly to the right. But despite the broken windowpanes and peeling paint, it was easy to see the old house had been a showplace during her heyday.

An unexpected pang of…something hit him—regret maybe?—while he stared at the exterior. Though he hadn't touched a hammer since the last time he'd visited his grandfather—almost a year ago, he realized, startled by how much time had gotten away from him—he suddenly had the lunatic urge to start in on repairs. Replace the rotten wood, level up the foundation, strip away the blistered paint and apply a glossy new coat of antique white. It could be beautiful again, Mick thought, as a corrected mental image of the old home surfaced in his mind.

A carpenter by trade, Charlie Chivers certainly hadn't let those summers Mick had spent with him go to waste. While no one would ever mistake Mick for a master carpenter, he knew his way around a toolbox, and had always taken great pride in helping his grandfather with his work.

Frankly, he'd always looked forward to those summers, learning better ways to repair and build. At the end of the day, he'd never failed to be pleasantly exhausted and proud of what he'd accomplished. Though he could say the same for every successful mission he'd made for Uncle Sam, Mick had to admit the levels of satisfaction had been…different. One hadn't been any better than the other, but they certainly hadn't been the same.

Funny. Until now he'd forgotten about how much he'd enjoyed the weight of a hammer in his hand, the weariness in his muscles at the end of the day.

"It's a shame, isn't it?" Sarah Jane asked, as though reading his thoughts.

Mick felt a sigh slip past his lips. "Yeah," he said slowly. "A total waste. What happened?"

"The usual. Lack of finances." She shrugged. "One drought too many. The family ultimately scattered, each pursuing their own dreams." She gestured to the land surrounding the house. "It takes more than a few folks to run a farm this size. People have smaller families now, so there's less help and less money. Eventually the bank foreclosed and Ervin Manus bought the place at auction on the courthouse steps for less than the cost of a new car." The note of bitterness in her voice was unmistakable. "The house is scheduled for demolition in a couple of weeks. He's putting in a dirt bike track out here. Says the landscape is perfect."

Damn, Mick thought. He'd been wrong. It was more than a waste—it was criminal.

"It took a lot of fast-talking to get him to agree to let me salvage the place first," she continued. Her lips twisted into a forced smile. "He didn't want me messing up his 'dozer schedule.'"

Mick inclined his head. "Ah, well. You wouldn't want to get between a man and a bulldozer, that's for sure."

"Ervin's a cretin," Mason remarked in disgust. For some reason the boy put Mick in mind of an overweight Shaggy from the Scooby-Doo cartoons. "But you can bet that will never happen again. We put every bank and all of the corresponding county clerk's offices in a hundred mile radius on notice."

"I would have bought it myself had I known," Sarah Jane explained at Mick's puzzled look.

Surprised, he arched a brow. "For yourself?"

Though she didn't sigh, Mick watched her shoulders droop a bit. Sarah Jane looked up at the house, her unreadable gaze still hidden behind those damned sunglasses. She finally turned to him and, shrugging slightly, smiled. He felt the impact of that casual grin resonate oddly through him. "To tell you the truth, I don't know. I just hate to see it destroyed. Renovated, this house and property would make a lovely home for a family." She kicked at an errant rock at her feet. "Knowing that it's going to be razed to the ground and a dirt track put in its place, frankly, makes me sick to my stomach."

Him, too, and he shouldn't give a damn. About the house, or about how losing it made her feel. He wasn't here to care. Until he learned otherwise, he was here to do a job for Chastity Walker, and nothing more. He was here because he'd almost gotten a man killed, because Huck had taken pity on him and gotten him a damned job Mick wasn't sure he even wanted, one he knew he didn't deserve.

He was here because his life was in shambles and he couldn't afford another screwup.

Mick took a couple of steps, lifted his camera and pulled Sarah Jane's intriguingly beautiful profile into focus, framing the first shot of his target.

She was that, dammit, and nothing more. He'd do well to keep *that* in focus.

SARAH JANE SNEAKED through the back door into Clara's kitchen just as Tina was smacking Chase's hand away from a take-out container. "That's not for you," she admonished.

Tall, blond and gorgeous, with a dimpled cheek and baby-blue eyes, Chase smiled, looking wounded, and shot Tina one of those slaying glances that never failed to make her friend melt. "What? You didn't save me a plate?" He lowered his voice an octave. "You know I love your lasagna."

"Yeah, well, so do I," Sarah Jane said, before her friend could swoon. She wearily dropped her purse onto the worn butcher-block counter and took a seat at the little antique table reserved for back-door guests. "Back off, buddy. You should have called her." It was a jibe with double meaning and, judging by the uncomfortable look on Chase's face, he knew it.

Tina blinked, seeming to come out of a trance. She huffed an exasperated breath and jerked her head toward the table. "Sit down," she said, predictably relenting. "I'll share mine with you." She shot him a look. "But you can pour your own tea."

A wry smile tugged at the corner of Chase's mouth. "You're a hard woman, Tina," he said, sauntering over to the pitcher on the counter.

Tina heaved a put-upon sigh. "Shut up or I'll change my mind."

Doubtful, they all knew, but it was fun watching the exchange. Tina had been in love with Chase for as long as Sarah Jane could remember. And Chase, while notoriously set on remaining single, couldn't seem to make up his mind who to spend time with, Tina or Laura Irving, one of Chastity's best friends, who had a similar set of big breasts and the same questionable morals. Laura delighted in keeping Chase on the line, and would occasionally reel him in just for the sport of it.

More than anything, it bothered Sarah Jane to see her friend continue to hold out hope for a relationship she wasn't all too sure would ever materialize beyond what it was—flirtatious banter punctuated with the occasional night of hot sex. In her opinion, it was time for Chase to fish or cut bait. In fact, if he didn't do one or the other in the near future, she'd more than likely tell him so.

Sarah Jane was sweet like that.

Tina retrieved another plate from the cupboard, along with some silverware and, though a faint smile curved her mouth and a blush of pleasure tinged her cheeks, grudgingly set them before Chase.

Sarah Jane repressed a grin and helped herself to a steaming square of lasagna. A groan of pure pleasure escaped as she tasted the creamy ricotta and marinara mixture.

Chase quirked an evil brow. "So that's what does it for you, eh?"

She rolled her eyes, enjoying her dinner. "Shut up," she said. "Honestly, is sex the only thing you men ever think about?"

He took a sip of tea, then leaned back and scratched his chest. Probably because scratching his balls would have been rude, Sarah Jane thought, suppressing a laugh.

"Nope. We think about football, too."

Ignoring Chase, Tina turned to her, and Sarah Jane knew before she even opened her mouth what was coming. "Speaking of doing it for you, I saw your photographer come in this afternoon."

The "ooh-la-la" wasn't spoken, but it was implied enough to cause Chase's gaze to sharpen. His fork stalled halfway to his mouth. "Photographer? What photographer?"

Heat scorched Sarah Jane's ears and thighs simultaneously at the mere thought of Mick Chivers. Of those mouthwatering shoulders and that intensely carnal mouth, specifically.

Rather than admit that she'd been in a state of bone-melting arousal all day, she told herself the one-hundred-degree-plus heat must have made her entire system malfunction. This low hum in her belly and persistent tingle between her legs was the result of dehydration, extreme heat and the general lack of sex in her life. She was having such a strong reaction to Mick because he was new, interesting and—because she hadn't been able to resist a little prying—single.

All those factors combined had tangled around her

woefully deprived libido, taken one look at Mick and gone haywire.

Logically, she knew all of this.

But attraction was rarely logical, and Sarah Jane knew no matter how many times she tried to convince herself—or how many excuses she made for her bitch-in-heat behavior—the outcome would be the same.

Simply put, she was in lust.

To the nth degree.

She glumly cleared her throat. "Oh? He's settled in, then?"

Tina snorted. "The man doesn't look like he ever 'settles,' but if you mean 'Has he checked into a room,' then the answer is yes." She shot Sarah Jane a reproachful look. "Why didn't you tell me he was gorgeous when you called?"

Chase scowled. "Gorgeous?"

Tina ignored him. "Do we need to go over the Need to Know rules again?"

Sarah Jane chuckled. She and Tina had started a list of Need to Know rules in high school, and the list had been growing ever since. So far they included, but weren't limited to the following:

1) All Gossip (Juicy or Otherwise)
2) Any Sighting of a Good-looking Boy
3) Cheating Boyfriends
4) Foreign Objects Stuck in Teeth
5) Any Clothing That Makes the Wearer Look Fat
6) Things That Make You Say "Hmm" (ordinarily covered by Rule #1)

7) Life-altering Decisions or Events
8) Sex (Having It or the Lack Thereof)

Ideally, two more rules would crop up, thus giving them the Ten Commandments of their friendship, but so far the eight they currently had in place covered everything.

Sarah Jane smiled. "Sorry," she said. "I didn't think about it." She braced herself, ready for the bolt of lightning that should have struck her for that whopping lie.

"Didn't think about him being gorgeous, or didn't think about telling me?"

"Again with the gorgeous." Chase chuckled darkly and hacked off another chunk of pasta. "Beating that horse to death, aren't you, Tina?"

She glared at him. "I thought you were hungry."

"I am."

"Then eat and let us talk, for pity's sake." She huffed another breath, then met Sarah Jane's gaze once more. "So?" she prodded, back to the interrogation at hand. "What did you think of him?"

Sarah Jane felt her face flame, which seemed appropriate considering Mick had unwittingly set the rest of her body on fire. "I thought he was gorgeous," she admitted with a sigh and felt a slow telling smile slide over her lips. *And I thought I wanted to suck him up like a Slurpee, personally investigate every inch of his spectacular body, sink my teeth into that marvelous ass and feel that wicked, supremely carnal mouth of his kissing the small of my back...and other places.* A chill ran through her, but did nothing to cool her down. Just the contrary, in fact.

And those were the *least* depraved things that had gone through her head today while she covertly studied her on-site photographer. Good Lord, just watching the man move made her want to whimper.

And Tina was right—Mick Chivers didn't look like he ever settled down. Though Sarah Jane had noticed it the minute he got out of his car, the impression had been repeatedly confirmed throughout the day. He never stopped moving.

Ever.

He was adjusting settings on his camera, inspecting the house, jiggling his leg. Being still seemed completely out of his area of expertise, and though he'd thought tearing down a house to build a dirt track was a shame, he'd later mentioned he wouldn't mind doing a little racing. That comment had led to several, in which he'd revealed that he loved skydiving, had dabbled in mountain climbing and basically enjoyed any sport that might result in death or bloodshed.

Because she was insane, Sarah Jane had found this fearlessness intensely sexy.

Tina let out a little squeal of delight and smacked her hand against the table. "OhmyGod! You want him. Oh, sweetie, I'm so happy for you! It's been such a long time since you—"

"Tina!" Mortified, she jerked her head in Chase's direction. "Do you mind?" Honestly, Monarch Grove was a small town—certainly too small and domestic for someone like her new photographer, she thought glumly—so her lack of a sex life was pretty much common knowledge. Still…

Chase grinned, leaned back and crossed his arms over

his chest. "I don't mind in the least. You ask me, this shit is fascinating. You're blushing, Sarah Jane," he said, seemingly amazed, his blue eyes twinkling with undisguised interest. "I don't think I've ever seen you do that."

That's because she ordinarily *didn't* blush. It was completely out of character for her. Much like this otherworldly attraction to Mick she had going on. Had she ever lusted? Certainly. But not to this degree. With a single half smile, this guy had managed to make her simultaneously jittery and muddled, hot and achy, wet and on fire.

"You're interrupting again," Tina said, exasperated. "Either be quiet or go home," she snapped, using her Italian "Obedience or Death" tone. She gestured to Sarah Jane and dragged her chair closer. "Can't you see we're trying to talk?"

Still smiling, Chase feigned contrition and didn't say anything else.

"So?" Tina prodded.

Sarah Jane shrugged. "So…what?" And that was it in a nutshell. "He's the photographer for the piece *Designing Weekly* is doing on my company, and we both know I need the business too much to muck it up by—" she paused, unable to come up with the proper description for what she'd like to do with Mick Chivers "—you know," she said, gesturing wearily.

"Screwing around," Chase interjected helpfully.

Mildly annoyed, Sarah Jane propped her chin in her hand and stared at him. "You're enjoying yourself, aren't you?"

"Hell, yeah," he readily admitted, a broad grin splitting his face. "The only thing that could make this any better would be a beer and a bowl of popcorn. It's nice to see a woman in lust for a change. You females are always harping about us guys, about us not having any *self-control* and giving in to our *animal urges* and all that crap," he said with a derisive grimace. He suddenly brightened. "Seeing the shoe on a smaller foot is a refreshing change. If I see Mr. Gorgeous—" he shot a pointed look at Tina "—I think I'll thank him." Chase stood, then pressed a kiss to her cheek, making her sag in her chair. "Thanks for dinner, Tina," he murmured. "It was wonderful, as always."

Tina waited until he was gone, then sighed. "No promise to call this time," she said, her big eyes haunted with melancholy.

Sarah Jane inwardly winced. She'd noticed. "Sorry, Tina. But it's better than having him lie to you, right?"

"I suppose."

"You know what I think," she reminded her gently.

"I do. But finding someone else isn't that easy."

Sarah Jane couldn't imagine loving someone who didn't love you back was any easier, but kept that opinion to herself. Tina had no illusions where Chase and his mysterious feelings were concerned. Frankly, Sarah Jane thought a little friendly competition—he'd certainly been jealous enough over the "gorgeous" comment a few minutes ago—would make the wily boy in blue sit up and take notice. At the moment, he knew Tina adored him and was a sure thing. He wasn't about the change the status quo. A little uncertainty would undoubtedly do him some good.

"So...back to your photographer," Tina said. "Just because he's here on business doesn't really mean he's off-limits, does it?" she asked with skeptical hopefulness. "He's made you blush. *You.* Ms. Unflappable. Ms. Hard-ass."

"I am not a hard-ass," Sarah Jane retorted automatically, though, to an extent, she imagined it was true. She'd never been one to suffer fools gladly—stupid behavior drove her crazy—and she didn't mince words. She'd never mastered the coy art of guarding her tongue or dancing around an issue. It was a waste of time that, more often than not, resulted in confusion.

At any rate, she imagined the only thing that saved her from being labeled a total bitch was her notoriously soft heart, which she would freely admit to owning. She was a sucker for a sob story, a constant champion of the underdog, and had never met a stray she hadn't kept or, at the very least, found a home for.

Oh, yeah, she thought, remembering the half-dozen furry family members waiting for their kibble, she was a real hard-ass.

As for whether or not Mick was really off-limits, the answer, though difficult to make, was a resounding yes.

She'd been wrestling with that question and her damn attraction to the man all day.

"Don't think I'm not tempted, and don't think my being around him for the next two weeks isn't going to be sheer hell—it is. But he's here in a professional capacity and, bottom line, I need the business and exposure from the article more than I need an orgasm."

Tina grinned. "I think you need the orgasm worse."

"Will your opinion pay my bills?"

"No, but your inheritance would," Tina quipped. "Any luck with Cecil this morning?"

Sarah Jane felt her neck cramp. "None."

Which was all the more reason she needed to forget about the unforgettable sex she might have had with Mick Chivers—everything within her wailed and rebelled at this thought—and concentrate on the issues at hand.

Frankly, getting her hands on that will and seeing this article through were more important than a weeklong fling with the best-looking, sexiest man she'd ever seen. Mick's handsome face—more specifically, that beautiful mouth and what he could no doubt do with it *to her*—rose in her mind's eye, making her inwardly wince with bone-deep regret.

No doubt the fling would be more satisfying.

But it wouldn't buy her a new truck.

4

"So, HOW'S IT GOING so far?" Huck asked. Evidently, he was the one assigned to check up on him. Or, Mick supposed, Huck could be doing it independently, trying to make sure that he didn't botch his first job. He'd recommended Mick, after all, ergo his credibility was on the line, as well.

Swallowing a sigh, and unable to shake the sensation that he was being watched, Mick closed his bedroom door, locked it and pocketed the key, holding his cell phone to his ear the whole time. He'd also smelled a strange sort of aftershave when he'd awoken this morning—and it hadn't been his. Very weird. "No illegal activity last night," he told Huck.

Under the pretense of "getting a feel for the town" Mick had done an open tail—meaning he'd allowed his quarry to see him, but had kept enough distance between them that she hadn't been aware he'd actually been following her. Furthermore, because the community was so small and everything of interest was centered around the town square or within a couple of blocks, running into her repeatedly hadn't caused any suspicion. In addition, he planned to always keep his camera with him from now on and use it as a prop when necessary.

As for her movements last night, she'd had dinner here with a friend—Tina Martinese, the B and B chef, who'd provided him with some of the best lasagna he'd ever eaten in his life—then drove by Chastity's house, but didn't stop.

Afterward she'd driven past the town limits and, after about ten minutes, turned down a long tree-lined driveway. Mick wouldn't have been able to follow her without it looking odd, so he'd doubled back and waited for her to make the return trip to town. Whoever she'd visited couldn't have asked her to stay, because she'd been back on the road within twenty minutes. After her mysterious stop—one he fully intended to check out later—she'd dropped by the local video store and then gone home.

There she took a damn long time in the shower— long enough to make him want to howl, actually. Then she put on a tiny cotton camisolelike thingie—no bra, of course, because she evidently wanted to kill him— and a pair of boxer shorts, dished up a bowl of ice cream, curled up on her couch with her assorted menagerie of pets and watched a movie.

He'd kept her under surveillance until he was certain—or as certain as he could be—that she was in for the night. He'd finally made it back to the B and B around two-thirty, only to set off some sort of alarm that woke the entire house, including Clara—whose hair, interestingly, had gone from red to blond sometime between supper and his return. She grudgingly gave him the security code to disarm the system, but only after he'd told her that he suffered from insomnia and would more than likely need to take a walk *every* night.

His cheeks burned as he remembered that humiliation. He was only glad that none of his counterparts had seen or heard it. *Badass security specialist at your service,* he thought with a sardonic twist of his lips, wondering if he could possibly screw this up any more.

At any rate, he'd gotten very little sleep and had nothing to show for his efforts but a dull headache, a general sense of uneasiness—he could have sworn he'd felt a hand on his thigh this morning when he'd woken up—and an attack of conscience the likes of which he'd never experienced in his misbegotten life.

Mick paused on the landing before going downstairs to breakfast. "I gotta tell you, Huck. I feel like a first-class bastard."

"What do you mean?"

"I mean the cover I'm using." He leaned against the wall, checked to make sure he was alone and massaged the bridge of his nose. "Did you know that she's spent the last week busting her ass to get her inventory accounted for and uploaded onto her Web site, so she'll be prepared for the influx of business she's expecting to pick up because of this article? The one that's *not* going to happen?"

Huck paused, then muttered a curse. "No, I didn't."

"I know that I don't work for her, and I'm not supposed to care, but evidently I'm not as much of a son of a bitch as I'm supposed to be because I think this is pretty damn shitty."

Messing with a person's livelihood was *not* cool.

Monumental screwup aside, Mick had been more than a spectator for justice. He'd been a contributor. Disarming terrorists, fighting for the greater good, ensuring freedom—those were things he'd always been able to be proud of.

He wasn't proud of this.

There was no greater good, just greater greed on the part of Chastity Walker. Or at least, that's what he suspected at the moment.

"You're right," Huck said. "I'll see if I can do something about it."

"What could you do?"

"Maybe get them to run an article. And if I can't, I'm certain that Payne can." Huck chuckled softly. "He…has a way of getting people to do things us mere mortals can't."

Mick laughed. "That way is called *money,* my friend." He'd heard rumors of Payne's wealth for years, but could honestly say he'd never fully appreciated the depth of the man's pockets until he'd walked into the sleek Atlanta high-rise that housed Ranger Security, not to mention the additional building next door Payne had acquired and turned into apartments for future Ranger Security operatives. When Mick had stepped into his fully furnished right-down-to-a-stocked-pantry apartment, he'd been forcibly reminded of why Payne's friends had nicknamed him The Specialist.

The man did *nothing* in half measures.

"I know you don't like the cover, Mick, but we'll make it right. You just do what you're supposed to do and keep snapping pictures. You can give them to the magazine when you're through."

Feeling marginally better about it, Mick released a small breath. "All right." Taking photos of his target certainly wouldn't be a hardship. Sarah Jane wasn't a classic beauty by any stretch of the imagination. Her nose was a little too small, her cheeks too round, but he couldn't deny that he'd been drawn to her from the beginning. It was that fighter's spirit obvious in the stubborn tilt of her chin, that underlying hint of mischief evident in those melting-caramel eyes. In fact, it was those very characteristics that made her all the more compelling. She was sexy and salt-of-the-earth personified, an intriguingly irresistible combination.

"I heard from McPherson last night," Huck said. "He mentioned he'd tried to call you, but hasn't had any luck. Is there any particular reason you're avoiding him?"

Other than the fact that he was a coward who couldn't bear to talk to a friend who'd witnessed the biggest mistake of his life, no, Mick thought, feeling like a bastard. Rather than answer, he evaded the question. "I'll, uh…I'll give him a call." And he would. He just didn't know when.

"Make sure you do, man. He's worried about you."

Mick didn't need the reminder. A fellow adrenaline junkie and prankster, Levi McPherson was a good friend, one who, like Huck, had been there to rally around him when he'd screwed up. He hadn't tried to belittle Mick's regret with the standard it's-not-your-fault platitudes, but had been there to drink, to listen and offer sports-related therapy. The guilt was Mick's cross, not his. Levi didn't deserve the silent treatment Mick had been giving him.

Another screwup, he thought, disgusted with himself.

"And I should warn you," Huck said, thankfully changing the subject. "Chastity has called here several times asking for your cell number. She wants to meet with you to go over the case."

His gut response was a heartfelt *hell no,* but considering he'd already lost all perspective—provided he'd ever had it to start with—he didn't altogether trust his instincts. "I know that I'm new to this whole security thing, but is that a risk we should take?"

"Not in my opinion, but she's adamant. She's looking for you."

Mick grimaced. "Considering this is the only place to stay in town, I'm definitely easy to find."

Huck's hesitation echoed over the line. "Are you sure you're good with this, Mick? If you aren't, we can pull you out and give it a little more time. None of these guys would blame you. They've—"

Shame burned through Mick. Huck had stuck his neck out for him, had given him a place in the world when his life was in shambles. It still was, for that matter. "I can do it, Huck," he insisted. It was a simple mission. Watch Sarah Jane.

"No one's saying you can't, Mick. Hell, man, you're the best damn soldier I know. Freaking fearless. You're The Hell-raiser," he said with a reminiscent chuckle. Huck sighed, seemingly looking for the right way to tell Mick he was a fuckup. "But I can tell your heart's not in this."

Mick couldn't deny that, so he didn't even try. The only thing his heart had ever truly been in was serving his country, and that life was gone now, lost to him through nobody's fault but his own. A single bad decision that had come within a couple of centimeters of costing another man his life. Risk came with the job, he knew, and the higher up the chain of command you were, the more responsibility you had. In theory, he'd been fine with it. But living with the reality of the mistake had turned out to be more than he could handle. If that made him weak, then he could live with it easier than he could the alternative.

Risking his own life was one thing. Risking someone else's was another thing altogether.

Still, though he admittedly saw more shades of gray than black and white, he couldn't shake the sensation that he was fighting on the wrong side on this one. It didn't matter that Chastity was paying for their services—quite possibly with Sarah Jane's inheritance—it still felt off. And he had every intention of finding out why. If Chastity was using Ranger Security for something other than what she'd claimed when she'd hired them, Mick would find out and adjust his plan accordingly.

And she might not like the result.

While it was true that soldiers were taught to follow orders and respect the chain of command, they were also taught to assess situations, think on their feet and change course should the need arise. Furthermore, concepts like truth and honor and justice weren't just pretty words bandied about by politicians—they were a moral code. When in doubt, do what's right.

Mick assured Huck he would stay on task, thanked him for the heads-up regarding Chastity, then disconnected and finished making his way downstairs.

The heavy scents of bacon and maple syrup flavored the air, making his mouth water in anticipation. When

Payne had mentioned that Clara's was the hot spot for breakfast, he hadn't exaggerated. The dining room, a charming space littered with mismatched tables and chairs, fresh-cut flowers and braided rugs, was packed with people. Old farmers sporting overalls and John Deere hats, young professionals, couples and families, a hungry sample of Monarch Grove's population all gathered at the altar of good food.

Wearing a little tiara on her new platinum locks, and bright red lipstick, Clara greeted Mick herself before showing him to a table. "I hope you were able to sleep after your walk," she said, a polite, unintentional reminder that he'd woken them all up. He smiled and resisted the urge to grind his teeth.

"I was, thank you," he answered, settling into a chair.

"Nothing strange happened, I hope? No missing toiletries or flickering lights?"

"Er…no." He was caught off guard by the strange question.

Instead of looking happy, Clara actually seemed disappointed. Her face fell. "Excellent," she murmured distractedly.

Mick decided a subject change was in order. "If breakfast is as good as it smells, then I'm in for a treat."

She brightened. "You definitely are. Tina's a phenomenal cook. She's my little ace in the hole. The B and B has the best food in town, no matter what anyone tells you." She leaned down as though about to share an important secret. "Steer clear of Mabel's Diner," she whispered. "She's had a bit of a bug problem, if you catch my drift."

Mick inclined his head, wondering why Clara sounded slightly gleeful.

The woman straightened once more. "Coffee?"

"Er...black, please."

She nodded briskly and hurried away.

Clara hadn't been gone five seconds before a busty blonde who looked as if she'd colored her extremely tanned face with a paint-by-numbers kit suddenly slid into the chair across from him.

Chastity, no doubt, Mick decided, inwardly recoiling.

While attractive in the literal sense, she had a hard, cunning look about her. Though she wore black, the tight sleeveless shirt and short skirt hardly said "grieving widow." More like "streetwalker," he thought uncharitably.

She and Sarah Jane couldn't have been more different, and if he hadn't trusted this woman's story to begin with, he sure as hell didn't believe it now.

"You must be Mick," she said, smiling. Feminine interest sparkled in eyes surrounded by clumps of mascara-coated lashes.

"I am."

When he didn't say anything else, a momentary look of confusion stole across her overly made-up face. "So?" she prodded. "How are things going?"

"Fine. When I have something to report, I'll tell you. Wasn't that the agreement?" He purposely kept his tone level, knowing that any interest or even superficial friendliness would only encourage her to stay.

"I'm not sure," she replied slowly. Those shrewd eyes continued to size him up. She hesitated. "Is there a problem, Mr. Chivers?"

Mick swallowed a long-suffering sigh. More problems than he cared to enumerate.

Thankfully, a petite, dark-haired woman—Tina, maybe?—came to his rescue by arriving with his plate. "Good morning," she said, smiling warmly at him. "I'm Tina," she confirmed. She didn't so much as glance at Chastity. "You're the photographer who's working with Sarah Jane, right?"

From the corner of his eye he saw Chastity's lips slide into a smug smile. Though it went against everything inside of him, he managed to nod, silently affirming the lie.

He was *so* not cut out for this line of work.

Or maybe it was just this case. Either way, he knew he was screwed. And though he'd been in the security field for only a couple of days, that was long enough for Mick to know it wasn't going to satisfy his soul. The job entailed lots of watching and less movement, and other than actually being with Sarah Jane, it was a complete bore.

"We didn't get a chance to meet last night. I've got your to-go order ready in the kitchen, so don't forget to ask for it on your way out."

"I won't, thanks."

Chastity cleared her throat loudly. "Aren't you going to take my order?"

Every muscle in Tina's petite body went rigid and she turned a patently false smile in Chastity's direction. "I'm not a waitress. I'm the cook."

"Nevertheless, you work here and I'm a paying customer. I'd like what he's having."

"Fine," she said, baring her teeth in a frightening smile. "I'll make something *special* for you."

Only if spit were special, Mick thought, resisting

the urge to laugh. Evidently Chastity wasn't as stupid as she looked, because she finally just let out a disgusted breath and told her to forget it.

Victorious, Tina grinned. "Are you sure? I'd be happy to personally take care of your plate. Really," she said through clenched teeth. "I would."

"I said no," Chastity repeated. She gestured impatiently to Mick. "Can't you see you're interrupting our conversation?"

Tina's expression turned shrewd and speculative. "You know each other?"

Dammit to hell, this was exactly what he'd been afraid of. "We just met," Mick said, thankful that he hadn't had to lie again.

Seemingly satisfied, she nodded. "Enjoy your breakfast, Mick." She moved away from the table, giving him a clear view of the door.

He wished she hadn't.

Because Sarah Jane was standing there. An instantaneous frisson of heat stole through his belly and settled in his loins at the mere sight of her.

But it was the sight she was going to get—of him seated with her enemy—that worried him.

A sardonic, knowing smile rolled over her lips, as though she'd hoped he'd have better taste. She gave him a little nod in acknowledgment, then looked away.

Following his gaze, Chastity glanced over her shoulder, saw Sarah Jane, then, smiling maliciously, stood.

"Mission accomplished," she said. "Watch her like a hawk and let me know the minute you catch her breaking into my house. I'm looking forward to sending her back to jail."

"SHE DIDN'T WASTE MUCH time, did she?" Mason muttered under his breath. "I swear I think that woman has got some sort of sonar for when new men arrive in town. It's like a 'fresh meat' alarm goes off and she swoops in, ready for the kill."

Seething, reeling and bitterly disappointed, Sarah Jane nodded to a couple of people as she walked through the dining room, paused to listen to Mae Bell Hodges's latest update on her husband's gout, then continued on to the kitchen, where she and Mason typically ate breakfast with Tina.

Though she knew it was irrational and more than likely simply a product of her sexually deprived, lust-ridden brain, Sarah Jane's internal alarms were ringing so loudly she could barely hear her own thoughts.

Something about seeing Mick Chivers with Chastity was…off.

And it was more than the absurd jealousy and illogical anger turning her mind first shades of green, then black. It didn't have anything to do with the fact that she'd actually applied a little makeup this morning, had taken time with her hair and had agonized over which friggin' shorts made her ass look smaller. If Chastity was Mick's type—cheap, easy and stupid—then so be it. Good riddance. She shoved open the kitchen door with a little more force than needed, almost crashing into Clara.

"Sarah Jane," the woman admonished, adjusting the little crown on her newly tinted hair. "That's not how a lady enters a room. This is a bed-and-breakfast, not a roadhouse bar."

"Sorry, Clara." She dropped into a chair at the

kitchen table, snagged a biscuit from the tray and took an intentional bite to keep from screaming.

Tina sent her a sympathetic smile. "You saw."

"She did," Mason said, because Sarah Jane's mouth was still stuffed with food. He shook his head. "You know, I'm a man and even I don't get it. Yes, the girl has got a nice set of breasts—"

Sarah Jane glared at him.

"She does, S.J. Just stating the facts." He frowned, his peach fuzz bunching around his lips. "But there's nothing else there. She's not ugly, but she's not beautiful, either. She's spent so many hours in the tanning bed—"

"And by the pool she talked my father into putting in," Sarah Jane interjected.

"—she looks like a damn rotisserie chicken. She's dumb as a box of rocks." He shrugged again. "I just don't get it."

Tina set a steaming plate in front of each of them, grabbed one for herself and then joined them at the table. "You're just a man of better taste, Mason," she said. "Unfortunately, a lot of guys don't care whether a woman is smart or not." She shot a look at Sarah Jane. "No offense to your father, but he couldn't have been thinking with his brain when he decided to marry that shallow, mean-spirited slut."

"I know," Sarah Jane admitted, though she believed that her father had come to regret it in the weeks prior to his death. He'd said a few things, but nothing that would have really opened an honest dialogue about the situation. Just enough to leave Sarah Jane with the impression that he hadn't been happy.

And she'd be lying if she hadn't hoped that Mick would have better taste. Honestly, physical attraction aside, she credited him with more character. He hadn't seemed like the type who would be interested in Chastity. Sarah Jane had thought he had more depth. More class. More sense.

Frankly, by yesterday afternoon, she'd thought she'd detected a little interest in *her.* While he hadn't blatantly flirted, he'd certainly been quick with those slow, melting smiles, and there'd been a hint of interest in those shockingly blue eyes. Honestly, she'd never seen eyes that particular shade before. Intense, clear, bold, the color of an old bottle she'd once found buried in the sand at the beach. And if it was true that the eyes were indeed the window to the soul, then Mick Chivers's soul was a kaleidoscope of recklessness, irreverence, honor, pain and sorrow. How did she know this?

The same way she knew there was more to Chastity and Mick than met the eye: intuition.

True, Chastity had a knack for picking up the scent of any new man, but from the strange look—a combination of irritation and embarrassment—Sarah Jane had glimpsed on Mick's face, something else was in play here.

"If it makes you feel any better, I was in the dining room when she came in. He didn't invite her to sit down. She invited herself," Tina offered.

Typical Chastity. Still…

"I've got a weird vibe about this," Sarah Jane said. She speared a fresh strawberry and considered it thoughtfully.

Tina selected a piece of bacon and snickered. "That feeling is called jealousy, my dear."

Mason's gaze widened. "Jealousy? What do you mean, jealousy?"

Tina merely rolled her eyes. "Mason, you are a sweetheart, but you're blind."

"These are new glasses," he said, offended, straightening a bit in his chair. "It's just taking me a little while to adjust to them."

Sarah Jane and Tina shared a look, then both started giggling.

Used to their silent communication, he quirked his lips. "Want to clue me in on the joke?"

"No," Sarah Jane said. She cleared her throat and glanced at Tina. "It's…more than what you said. This situation just doesn't feel right."

"Sarah Jane, it doesn't feel right because the woman has been the bane of your existence since kindergarten. She stole your father, stole your house, stole your inheritance, and now she's put the moves on the first guy who has cranked your tractor in months."

"It's been more like a year or two, thank you," Sarah Jane corrected glumly.

Mason's eyes rounded and he gazed at her in astonishment. "Oh," he said knowingly, shooting her a sheepish smile. "That explains a lot. I thought you were acting a bit funny yesterday. Strange, really. I just thought you were nervous over all those pictures he was taking of you."

That *had* been a bit nerve-racking. It seemed like every time she'd turned around, Mick had been snapping another photograph. It was also clear that he knew a bit about carpentry and home repair. He'd inspected the house and made a lot of comments regarding the structure and how it could be fixed. At one point, he'd even put his camera down long enough to help her loosen a particularly stubborn bit of molding. She could tell he'd been itching to do more, but she hadn't suggested that he pick up a hammer.

In her line of work—a predominantly male field— Sarah Jane battled against what she'd dubbed the "little woman syndrome." On more than one occasion, she'd dealt with a clod-brained, big-muscled moron who thought she was too weak and too ignorant to do the job, so she'd become a bit sensitive to help from the opposite sex. She glanced at Mason and felt her own lips twitch. He didn't count— *she* was manlier than he was. At any rate, if she were perfectly honest, she'd let Mick help her because she'd wanted to be closer to him, to watch those muscles bunch and tighten.

And she hadn't been disappointed at all.

The man was, in a word, *glorious.*

And he'd been sharing breakfast with Chastity.

Sarah Jane didn't care what Tina said, this feeling— this instinct—was more than jealousy. Though she would definitely cop to that. She'd planned on asking Mick to join them for breakfast this morning, so seeing him two feet from her enemy hadn't been pleasant.

"I asked them if they knew each other," Tina told her. "And he said they'd just met."

Rather than put her at ease, Sarah Jane felt her nape prickle. "Why would you ask that?"

"Because your stepmonster accused me of 'interrupting their conversation.'" She quirked a brow in irritation. "Have I mentioned lately that I loathe her?

Because I do. I genuinely can't stand her." Tina took a sip of orange juice and sighed.

"Welcome to the club," Sarah Jane said with a grimace.

"You know what I think you should do?"

Sarah Jane suspected she wasn't going to like Tina's advice. "What?"

"Forget this whole he's-off-limits-because-he's-here-on-business crap and flirt with him. Reel him in." She grinned and her eyes sparkled with evil humor. "It'll kill her."

Oh, it would, no doubt, Sarah Jane thought, tempted beyond reason. A little quickening thrill made her insides tingle with purpose, and she felt a slow smile slide across her lips as she imagined Chastity's furious face. Sarah Jane paused, remembering all the reasons she shouldn't make a play for Mick, the most important of which was her business. She couldn't discount the fact that pursuing any sort of relationship with him—especially one of the sexual variety—would be risky, even potentially disastrous.

But the idea of letting Chastity win—*again*—was almost more than Sarah Jane could bear.

It was galling.

It was exasperating.

It was…impossible.

"She's taken everything else from you," Tina said with a shrug, echoing Sarah Jane's own thoughts. "You're a fool if you let her have him, too."

"Sarah Jane's no fool," Mason remarked, outraged on her behalf. He was always coming to her defense, even when he didn't need to.

A beat slid into three, then she looked at Tina and felt a resolute smile curve her lips. "He's right. I'm no fool."

Competitive, maybe. Self-destructive? Possibly. But not foolish.

5

MICK DIDN'T KNOW what kind of greeting to expect from Sarah Jane after she'd seen him with Chastity that morning. A cold shoulder, the silent treatment, a dire warning about the company he was keeping. Those were the scenarios running in his brain as he'd driven out to the Milton Plantation after breakfast.

The one scene he *hadn't* pictured, however, was the one playing out before him now.

Sarah Jane Walker was *flirting* with him.

Ordinarily, a beautiful girl making a play for him—particularly this one, who had the singular ability to turn him on simply by breathing—would be a good thing. Hell, an unbelievably freakin' *great* thing.

He liked women. He loved sex. He was a man, after all, and like most men, he spent the majority of his time thinking about getting laid, getting into trouble and getting a bite to eat. A slow smile drifted over his lips.

And not necessarily in that order. But if they happened in quick succession, then all the better.

At any rate, Mick had decided that Sarah Jane's

interest had to be some sort of cosmic revenge for all the hell-raising and womanizing he'd done in the past. Too many pranks, too many one-night stands, too many "too manys." When karma decided to dole out a payback for almost getting Carson Wells killed, Mick had imagined it would be much more heinous than what he was about to go through with Sarah Jane.

Not that it would be a cakewalk, by any stretch of the imagination. He looked at her through the viewfinder, zoomed in on her mouth and felt his blood race to his groin as he snapped yet another picture that would never make it into the magazine spread. In fact, he could safely say that *Designing Weekly* wouldn't be interested in about ninety percent of the photos he was taking. His lips quirked.

He'd been taking more pictures of *her* architecture than that of this old house.

But he couldn't seem to help himself. The smooth shape of her jaw, the sensual slope of her neck, even the delicate shell of her ears seemed to be irresistible once he got behind the lens. He'd taken a couple of good shots of her mouth—the single most beautiful thing he had ever seen, period—and longed to capture her eyes, those compelling pools of melting toffee. Gorgeous, warm and expressive. A guy could easily get lost in them, Mick thought broodingly.

When he'd first noticed the change in her, he had chalked it up to wishful thinking. Which was stupid, considering that he couldn't touch her. Given the situation— that he was a paid spy who was technically supposed to be catching her doing something illegal—it was beyond insane to *wish* that she would flirt with him.

He might be The Hell-raiser, but even he wasn't reckless enough, dishonorable enough, that he would throw sex into this mix. His pranks had always run along the lines of shaving the eyebrows off a drunken friend, putting cling wrap beneath the toilet lid, and the one that had made him infamous at Mars Hill Academy, dismantling a Civil War-era cannon and reassembling it in the headmaster's office. Mick inwardly smiled, remembering. That one had been good, if he did say so himself.

Nevertheless, wanting her to want him was the physical equivalent of hell, because he couldn't have her. While reams of paper could be filled with lists of his shortcomings, a faulty moral compass wasn't one of them. Furthermore, while he knew he was supposed to keep a close eye on Sarah Jane for Ranger Security, he suspected sleeping with her would fall well beyond the bounds of protocol.

Ultimately, Mick had decided that he had to be mistaken. That she couldn't possibly be genuinely interested in him that way. She was merely being friendly. Southerners were notorious for their hospitality, after all. That had to be it, he told himself, hoping that if he repeated it often enough, it would be true.

But then, only moments ago, she'd blown his theory—his admitted self-delusion—all to hell and, as a result, he was teetering on the verge of hysterical laughter, skating the edge of some sort of breakdown.

He'd fought terrorists. He'd survived enemy fire. He'd disabled bombs.

And yet this hardworking, down-to-earth little spitfire had somehow managed to shoot a dart of fear straight into his heart with alarming accuracy. Why?

Who knew? He suspected it had something to do with his inappropriate, unnamed feelings, plus a healthy dose of self-preservation.

Allowing himself to act on this attraction would be wrong on more levels than he could count. Which was a crying shame, because he'd never—*never*—felt this bone-deep, driving, almost elemental need to put himself inside a woman. On a civilized level, he would imagine it was as advanced as clubbing her over the head, then dragging her away to his cave by her hair. Or peeing around her yard, marking his territory.

"Is something wrong with your sandwich?" Sarah Jane asked.

Mick blinked. "Er, no. It's excellent." And the bite of chicken salad she'd caught from the side of his mouth and fed him with her thumb had tasted even better. He felt his groin tighten, just thinking about it.

Mason set his sandwich down and grimaced un-comfortably. "Nothing's wrong with mine, either, but I can't eat it."

A concerned line emerged between Sarah Jane's brows. "Why not? What's wrong?"

He took a small sip of lemonade from his Star Trek thermos. "I'm feeling a little queasy."

"Do you think it's the heat? Have you gotten too hot?"

Mason slowly shook his head. "I don't think so. It hasn't been as warm today as it was yesterday. Maybe it's just something I ate."

"You've eaten the same things I have and I'm not sick. Come on," Sarah Jane said, standing up from the small folding table they'd set up in the corner of the old dining room. "I'll take you home. You don't need to be here."

"No," Mason protested, shaking his sweaty head. "I'll be all right. I just need a—"

Sarah Jane reached out and placed her hand on his forehead, then frowned. "You've got a fever. I'm taking you home."

His eyes widened in outrage. "How can you tell I've got a fever? It's almost a hundred degrees in here."

"I can just tell," she said, shoving the rest of her food into a bag, now fully in mother-bear mode. "Come on. Get your things together."

Mason looked as if he would like nothing better than to go home, but firmed his nonexistent chin and prepared another argument. "You don't have time to drive me home, Sarah Jane. This job is taking longer than we thought and time is running out. I'll be fine. I—"

"How about I do it?" Mick offered. "I could give you a ride," he said to Mason.

Sarah Jane's hopeful gaze swung to Mick's, unexpectedly pulling the breath from his lungs. "Really? You wouldn't mind?"

"Not at all." He shrugged, trying hard not to feel like her knight in shining armor. "You need to work. He needs to go home." Furthermore, it would give him some time alone with Sarah Jane—a blessing and a curse—but most importantly, it would give him the opportunity to see if she might open up to him about her father. He needed to know if there really was a will, and he couldn't ask her without tipping his own hand.

"I don't like you being out here by yourself, Sarah Jane. It's dangerous," Mason protested weakly.

Her gaze grew steely and her adorable chin lifted at that stubborn angle Mick had come to recognize.

"Mason, we've been over this before. I am perfectly capable of working alone. I did it for years before you came along. I am able, I am responsible and I am careful. I don't need a babysitter. You go home. I'll be fine."

From the beleaguered tone of her voice, Mick guessed this was an argument they'd had many times before. Though she probably wouldn't like to hear it, he actually agreed with Mason. They were in a remote area and a bit of danger was inherent in her profession. She worked with sharp tools, in old dilapidated houses that were almost falling down around her. One misplaced step on a rotten board could result in a broken ankle, or worse. Like it or not, accidents came with the job description, and being here alone wasn't altogether safe. It wouldn't be for anybody, not just her.

"I'll be coming back out," Mick announced. "I need to get a few more pictures."

"Are you sure?" she asked, quirking a brow. "You've taken quite a few today."

So she'd noticed, he thought, wondering if she suspected he'd been taking more photos of her than of their actual progress. He rubbed a hand over the back of his neck. "I'll need to catalog each phase of the process," he lied, hoping it sounded believable.

Evidently it did, because she nodded. "Okay, then." She smiled gratefully at him. "I really appreciate this. Uh, why don't you let me make it up to you by showing you around our fair city this evening? Give you the grand tour, so to speak."

Even better for the case, Mick thought, though on a personal level, he knew he was beyond screwed.

Because he grimly suspected this was going to be a date.

And while he was new to the security business, he was relatively certain he was not supposed to *date* his target. But then, the list of things he was not supposed to do or notice was already quite long.

For instance, he was not supposed to notice the fullness of her breasts beneath her cotton T-shirt, the way her shorts rode up on her rear when she bent over, or the delicate tendrils of hair clinging to the back of her neck. He wasn't supposed to want to suck her bottom lip, or taste that little patch of skin behind her ear, or stretch her out on a blanket beneath that huge oak tree in the front lawn. He wasn't supposed to imagine her naked and hot and writhing beneath him. He wasn't supposed to want to fill her belly button with ice cream and lick it up. He wasn't supposed to dream about eating blackberries from between her thighs or suckling her sex until she came.

And he sure as hell wasn't supposed to—and for his own personal sanity didn't need to—agree to go out with her. But that's exactly what he did. It was the only way he was ever going to glean all the facts he needed to move forward on the case. Payne had told him to assess and adjust as necessary.

This was necessary.

"Sure," he told her, mentally cursing himself. "That sounds great."

She smiled at him. "Don't eat," she said. "I'll treat you."

That was exactly what he was afraid of, Mick mused, imagining all the ways he'd love for her to treat him.

To a kiss, for starters, he thought, eyeing her unbelievably carnal mouth. Then to bare skin, to pouting nipples and welcoming thighs, to her tongue on his body and her hands wrapped around his dick. To soft sighs and screams of release. To breakfast in bed and a hot, shared shower. Then to more of the same. He released a shuddering breath as the ache in his loins reached maximum capacity, and he shifted, angling for any sort of relief.

It didn't come.

And he grimly suspected the only cure, ironically, meant *he* would have to.

SARAH JANE LOOKED at the dismal contents of her closet and repressed the growing urge to scream. Evidently bewildered by her uncharacteristic behavior, all three dogs and one of her cats sat at her feet, staring at the collection of denim and T-shirts, as well. She looked down at them, rolled her eyes and grinned, thinking about the picture they all undoubtedly made. "What do you say, guys? You see anything in there that says 'casually sexy'? Hmm?" Her shoulders sagged as she sighed heavily.

Note to self, Sarah Jane thought. *The next time you buy clothes, keep a man in mind as opposed to comfort.*

Okay, time to get a grip, she decided, selecting yet another pair of denim shorts and a red gingham sleeveless blouse. She wouldn't make the cover of *Vogue,* but she liked the way both items looked on her, and that was good enough, right? After all, he'd agreed to go out with her when she'd been wearing a pair of shorts and a T-shirt, dripping with sweat and covered in dirt. Despite her appearance, she knew he was attracted to her, and to say that knowledge made her inwardly squirm with joy would be a mild understatement. Sarah Jane gave another little eye roll.

Of course, after the way she'd practically thrown herself at him today, she didn't imagine she'd left him with any choice, she thought, mildly embarrassed at her transparent behavior.

She'd smiled, she'd laughed, she'd purposely stared at his mouth—and not-so-purposely, as well, because she couldn't seem to help herself. She'd brushed up against him. She'd offered him water. She'd caught a little piece of his sandwich from the side of his mouth and fed it to him with her thumb.

She'd made herself clear....

And he'd said yes.

Take that, Chastity, you bleached-blond, thieving bitch, Sarah Jane thought, mentally doing a little hoo-yah dance because she was going to win.

And thoroughly enjoy herself in the process.

Honestly, when his gaze had tangled with hers and his lips had closed around her thumb, gently sucking, she'd felt that little tug all the way down to the heart of her sex. She'd come within a gnat's ass of having an immaculate orgasm, a phenomenon she'd never experienced. In fact, she could honestly say that orgasms had been so few and far between, she was beginning to suspect they were like unicorns and mermaids, the stuff of fairy tales.

But they wouldn't be with him, Sarah Jane thought, releasing a shaky breath.

Mick Chivers had *that* look. That baby-I-could-rock-your-world-beyond-your-wildest-dreams, turn-you-inside-out-and-back-again, make-you-scream-the-Hallelujah-Chorus-until-your-eyes-roll-back-in-your-head-and-your-bones-melt look. It was in the wicked curve of that slightly crooked smile, written in the sloping sexiness of those heavy-lidded, electric-blue eyes. It was in the way he moved, unhurried yet determined. It was in every hard, perfectly proportioned, muscled inch of his body—sex appeal, satisfaction guaranteed.

No long-term warranty though, she was sure, because he had *that* look about him, as well. Aside from the fact that Monarch Grove didn't have enough excitement to satisfy Mick's acute sense of adventure—another point that had been hammered home again today when he'd mentioned he'd actually swum with sharks off the coast of Australia—Mick was entirely too restless, unsettled and a bit wild, she thought, once again reminded of a lonely mustang.

Only a woman looking to have her heart trampled would ever dream of trying to put a bit in that mouth, she decided, making a mental note to keep it in mind lest she make the fatal mistake of becoming emotionally attached. This was about physical attraction, about keeping him from Chastity and nothing more. Did Sarah Jane like him? Certainly. Mick was charming, funny and intriguing.

But he was also temporary—and more importantly…damaged.

Every person had a story, she knew, but for whatever reason, she suspected Mick's had recently taken a tragic turn. There were shadows lurking in those beautiful eyes, a guardedness that spoke of untold pain. What had happened to him? she wondered. Heartbreak? She didn't think so. Instinct told her it was more personal than that. Went deeper, further, than he'd ever let anyone plumb.

She shrugged into her top and tugged the hem into place.

Because she had the "fix it" syndrome, she'd like nothing more than to try to help him. Sarah Jane had always been that way. Champion for the underdog, righter of any wrongs within the scope of her power, she hated injustice of any sort. And that was why Chastity keeping her inheritance more than hurt her— it pissed her off to no end. It was the reason Sarah Jane fostered animals, her motivation in always adopting an "angel" from the tree at Christmas, why she made a point to befriend the friendless. She couldn't help herself. Being a "do-gooder" was hardwired into her DNA. Any time she saw a person in need, she had the inherent urge to help.

Mick Chivers needed help, but something told her coming to his aid would be to her own detriment, and any effort would be rebuffed. Better to let him tackle his own demons, she thought, knowing that was the prudent decision, if not the easiest.

A knock at her front door announced his arrival, causing a flock of nerves to wing through her belly. The dogs went wild and rushed to the entrance ahead of her. Sarah Jane checked her reflection once more in her bedroom mirror, deemed herself presentable, then released a pent-up breath and, pushing Perv—her biggest dog, of unknown origins—aside, opened the door.

To her embarrassment but not her surprise, Perv, true

to his namesake, immediately went forward and nudged her visitor in the crotch.

Mick grunted, taken aback, then chuckled uncomfortably. "Whoa there, buddy," he said, carefully moving the dog's head from his zipper. "I, uh…I don't know you well enough for that."

Sarah Jane smiled a bit fatalistically. "Mick, this is Perv. You can imagine how he got that name."

Mick continued to pat the dog's head as he glanced up at her. "I don't have to imagine," he said, amusement in his voice. "I've got intimate knowledge."

Grimacing, she opened the door a little wider, welcoming him in. "Move back," she admonished the dogs. "Let the man inside."

His hair was still wet and curling from a recent shower, and as he complied, she breathed in the smell of his aftershave. He earned points with her immediately by bending down and taking time to greet and pet each of her animals. The dogs lapped up the attention, while the cats looked on in curious distain. "You've got a whole little zoo here."

"I know," Sarah Jane said. "But I love them."

He looked up and quirked a brow. "Strays?"

She nodded, once again broadsided by the almost overwhelming urge to slide her fingers over his lips. His mouth was quite honestly one of the most beautiful things she'd ever seen. "P-perv was abused," she stammered, struggling to focus. "I, um, I volunteer at our local animal shelter on the weekends, just checking in on the animals, and was there when his owners dumped him. He was so bewildered, so pitiful." A droll smile tugged at her lips and she ran her hand over the dog's sleek back. "Despite his lamentable habit of shoving his nose into unsuspecting crotches, he's a sweet, loyal dog." She gestured toward another of her brood. "That's Wink. She's part beagle, part something else."

"Wink?"

"She's got a droopy eye," Sarah Jane explained. "It's part of her charm."

She pointed to the smallest of her canines and sighed. "And that's Spaz."

Upon hearing his name, the little dog started running in circles, leaped up on the couch, raced from end to end, then jumped back down and repeated the process.

Mick chuckled. "No explanation needed on that one, either."

"I've also got three cats—Winken, Blinken and Nod." She gestured to each in turn. "Their favorite pastime is sleeping, so their names fit."

"Quite a group," he said, smiling at her pets. "I've always wanted a dog."

Sarah Jane blinked, surprised. "You've never had one?"

Something dark shifted in his gaze. Then he sent her a sheepish grin that seemed more manufactured than sincere. "I was never home long enough," he said. "I spent most of my life in boarding school, then joined the military right after college." Another shadow clouded his eyes. "And with my current job, I'm gone for days at a stretch. It's not ideal circumstances for a pet." He smiled again, albeit awkwardly. "Maybe later."

Boarding school, then the military? Sarah Jane was a bit shocked and more than curious. She knew that boarding schools were more popular in the Northeast, but Mick definitely had a Southern drawl. Military school then? Had he been a problem child? Her gaze slid over that restless frame, the one that made her knees melt, and instinctively knew her guess could fit. Nevertheless, it seemed a bit harsh.

Though she hadn't given much thought to children—aside from wanting to have them at some point in her future—Sarah Jane couldn't imagine shipping them off, sending them away from home. What sort of parents had he had? she wondered. Robots? She remembered him mentioning that he'd spent summers with his grandfather, a little tidbit he'd shared today when she'd commented on his carpentry knowledge. So…if he'd spent months away at school and summers with his grandfather, just exactly *when* had he been home?

Nevertheless, the admission about being in the military fit. There was a precision in the way he did things, a confidence in the very way he moved that suggested some sort of specialized training. How long had he been in the service? she wondered. Which branch? And how did one make the leap from soldier to photographer? Though Mick obviously knew his way around a camera and was comfortable behind the lens, she had to admit, given his particularly brand of energy, it didn't seem the type of job a man like him would choose.

Interestingly, the only time he'd seemed to truly settle was this afternoon when she'd finally given in and handed him a hammer. He'd offered to help repeatedly, and between his pacing and snapping pictures, he'd generally been even more of a distraction than usual. But once he'd started helping her, he'd actually calmed down a bit and worked with impressive skill and attention to detail. He had an inherent ability, a respect for the architecture and an artisan's eye. Building a house was easy; saving pieces of one was a lot tougher. But Mick seemed born to this kind of work. She'd been pleasantly surprised, and for one ridiculous moment of wishful thinking, she'd had the strangest feeling that he belonged there with her.

Weird, Sarah Jane thought, refusing to entertain the idea, when she knew it was so far removed from actual possibility it was almost laughable.

It was much like her dream of ever owning Ponder Hill, she mused. That old mansion—now sitting empty, slowly turning to ruin despite her covert efforts to carry out a few repairs, owned by a mad old woman who refused to sell—had been the home she'd longed for since the instant she'd first laid eyes on it, when she was a little girl. Sarah Jane remembered that day as if it were yesterday. Making the long trip up the tree-lined driveway, seeing the gleaming white house on the hill. She'd been with her dad that day, working as his "assistant," though she'd barely been big enough to hand him a hammer, when he'd gone out to make a quick repair to one of the shutters.

Sarah Jane had fallen instantly in love with the house—the fancy windows, particularly a pretty stained-glass piece on the second floor; the sweeping porches; the beautiful courtyard. But more than anything, there was something about the way it had felt. The second her foot had connected with the hardwood in the foyer, she'd felt…home. As though the house had been waiting for her and she'd finally arrived. Even her childhood home on Maple Street—the one where

Chastity was currently living—had never felt as right to her as Ponder Hill. Any time her father had been called to do work on the old place, Sarah Jane had tagged along, eager for just a few minutes, however brief, to enjoy the home of her heart. She loved it there and, more than anything, wanted it.

Unfortunately, the current owner didn't possess what one would call a stable mind, and had no intention of selling it, or saving it from disrepair. Though Sarah Jane sneaked out and did what she could to keep it from getting any worse—repaired shingles, made sure the pipes were wrapped in the winter, those sorts of things—the years of neglect were slowly taking their toll. The place desperately needed rescuing.

Much like Mick, she thought, surprised at the strange revelation. He was an enigma, she decided, her gaze lingering on the masculine angle of his jaw, that smooth, perfect cheek. He was a riddle she wanted to solve…then taste.

He looked up at her and his gaze tangled with hers. A little zap of electricity sizzled in her nipples, shot through her belly and rested hotly in her sex. "Shouldn't we get going?"

Releasing a silent breath, Sarah Jane nodded. She made sure the animals were settled, then grabbed her purse and locked up. "Do you mind if I drive?" she asked.

A knowing half smile curled his lips. "Not if you don't mind if I take my camera."

"Not at all," she said. She climbed into her truck and waited for him to join her. "Though I don't know that you'll find anything of interest to photograph."

She heard a telltale click and turned just as Mick was

lowering the camera. His voice was low, almost intimate. "I already have."

Impossibly, Sarah Jane felt another blush rise on her cheeks. *Two for two,* she thought, wondering if she'd ever be the same.

"So…where are we going first?"

She grinned. "First we're going to take a little drive around the town square—" so that, with any luck, Chastity would see them, *muah ha ha* "—then we'll visit one of Monarch Grove's most interesting citizens, Carl Hirsch, better known more recently as Squatting Buck."

Mick chuckled and shook his head. "Why do I have a feeling this is going to be good?"

"Because it is."

And she hoped it was only going to get better.

6

RESISTING THE URGE to gnaw his tongue off after his "never had a pet" slipup, Mick settled into the passenger seat of Sarah Jane's truck and perused her house and front yard. A 1930s bungalow, the old Craftsman-style home sported a cozy porch swing and beautiful leaded glass in the front door. Purple and red petunias, golden marigolds and other flowers he couldn't name poured from eclectic pots and out of neat flower beds. Bird feeders, particularly those for hummingbirds, hung from various tree branches, and water in a little koi pond gurgled happily.

"You've got a nice place," Mick said. "Did you do the renovation yourself?"

She nodded. "My dad helped me. It wasn't in bad shape when I bought it, but it still needed a little TLC." Country music blared from the speakers when she cranked the ignition and, shooting him an adorably sheepish look, she quickly turned the stereo down before backing out of the driveway and making a right toward Main Street. "We, uh, we put in new cabinets, refinished the woodwork and floors, updated the bathrooms. My dad was a perfectionist in every sense of the word when it came to work," she said, laughing softly. "Mediocrity wasn't allowed, so everything was done right."

From all that Mick had seen, it certainly looked that way to him. And she'd obviously inherited the gene, because he hadn't seen a bit of subpar work in her repertoire. She was quick, careful and efficient, and it was painfully obvious that she loved what she did. He envied her that, he admitted, missing that part of his life. Not so much the Ranger days, but simply knowing his purpose. Mick felt like a ship without a rudder, adrift and directionless.

"I'm sorry for your loss," he told her, once again making a mental note to call his grandfather. Frankly, he didn't miss his parents—it was hard to miss people you never actually knew. But Charlie was different. And he wouldn't be around forever.

"Thank you," Sarah Jane murmured. "He was such a force of nature. It's still hard to believe sometimes that he's gone."

"Heart attack, right?" Mick asked, thankful that Mason had brought up the topic yesterday, which explained Mick's knowledge of it and enabled him to essentially avoid another lie.

"Yeah," she confirmed sadly. "One minute he was helping a buddy with a privacy fence, the next…" She shrugged, leaving the worst unspoken. "Anyway, it's been rough. My mom passed away when I was sixteen. Breast cancer," she added. "So being officially orphaned hasn't been easy to adjust to."

Mick had pretty much been in the same boat, so he understood exactly where she was coming from. "What about other family? Grandparents, aunts, uncles, cousins?"

"No grandparents. My mother was an only child, so no aunts or uncles on that side. My dad has a sister, but she lives in Little Rock. She came down for the funeral, of course, and I talk to her occasionally, but you know how it is." Sarah Jane released a little sigh. "Life gets in the way and, despite tragedy, it goes on."

So she had no real family to speak of, which explained her desire to hang on to her heritage—her father's pipe, her mother's wedding dress, her old home—not to mention the half-dozen pets that lived with her. She'd made her own furry family of sorts, clung to friendships and was determined to hang on to her past. Mick certainly couldn't fault her for that, once again feeling like a traitor in the friendly camp. He grimaced.

Probably because he was.

She hesitated and a wry smile curled her lips. "I actually have a stepmother, but considering she's stolen my home and inheritance, for obvious reasons, I don't count her." Sarah Jane laughed bitterly.

Mick felt his pulse quicken. At last. Maybe now he'd get some answers. "That's understandable," he said. This acting-and-lying thing was not for him. He hated pretending as if this wasn't old news, that he wasn't already familiar with every sordid detail of her troubles, that he might possibly be there to contribute to them. Though instinct was telling him that wasn't the case. In fact, he grimly suspected Chastity was using Ranger

Security to keep Sarah Jane from finding the will, as well as any personal mementos of her parents.

"You met her this morning," Sarah Jane added, her light tone at odds with the white-knuckled grip she had on the steering wheel.

He cleared his throat. "Oh?"

"The woman you were having breakfast with when I came in—Chastity."

Because he knew he was supposed to be surprised that her stepmother was her own age, Mick purposely widened his eyes in what he hoped was an appropriate expression of shock. This blew. Totally blew. "You're kidding! But she's—"

"—a money-hungry slut, I know," Sarah Jane finished.

He smothered a laugh and passed a hand over his face. God, she was wonderful. A beautiful hellion. "Actually, I was going to say, 'so young.'"

"That, too," she admitted. "We're the same age. Don't ask me what my father was thinking. I don't know." Her voice developed an edge. "I just know that she was never supposed to have the house and things that belonged to my mother."

Pay dirt. Tell me what I'm looking for, Mick thought. *Give me a reason to adjust my course. Let me help you.* "How do you know that?"

"Because, in what was the only sound decision that came out his lunatic marriage, Dad made out a will. He showed it to me because he didn't want me to worry." Her jaw worked. "But it has conveniently vanished from the filing cabinet where he kept it, as well as the copy at the attorney's office. Did I mention that my stepmonster is sleeping with the attorney?" she asked.

"Damn," Mick muttered, surprised at that last little tidbit. It was all he dared say. Furthermore, he had absolutely no doubt she was telling the truth. As part of his training, he'd taken several courses on body language and deceptive behavior. Sarah Jane's posture, word choice and story were right on target for the truth. He mentally relaxed and decided a new plan of action was in order. One that changed the status quo in Sarah Jane's favor.

"No worries," she replied, shooting him a determined smile. "I'm going to find it."

He knew she'd been planning this, but hearing her say it made him uneasy. While he admired her determination and would undoubtedly take the same approach if he'd been in her shoes, knowing that Chastity had gone so far as to hire them to keep Sarah Jane away made him a bit nervous.

"What are you going to do?"

"Get it back, of course."

"Have you tried going to the police?"

"It's my word against hers," Sarah Jane explained. "They can't do anything."

"But what about the attorney? Can't he verify that there is a will, even if he can't produce it?"

"He could, but he won't. He says it's been so long, he really can't remember drawing up a will for my father." She snorted. "He's lying, of course, but there's nothing I can do about it."

Maybe not, but *he* could, Mick thought, surprised at how much he wanted to track down this attorney and loosen a few of his teeth.

"Anyway, you should watch yourself," she said. "If

you get tangled up with Chastity, she'll suck the marrow right out of your bones."

Mick chewed the inside of his cheek, enjoying what he could only assume was jealousy on her part. "I'll keep that in mind. But to tell you the truth, she's not my type."

Seemingly pleased, Sarah Jane curved her lips in a smile, and it was utterly ridiculous how happy that little grin made him. It was so wonderful, in fact, that he wanted to do it again and again, wanted to make her laugh so that he could feel the sound resonate throughout his own chest. He was in dangerous waters, he realized, fearing he'd already ventured out over his head.

Though he didn't have any idea what the hell was going on with him—admittedly, his life was an absolute wreck—today, working with Sarah Jane, had been the happiest he'd been in recent memory. It had taken a good bit of convincing on his part to get her to agree to let him help her, but once he had, and they'd actually started working together, it had been the strangest thing.... The rest of the world—the constant need to move, his perpetual adrenaline craving—had simply faded away. Vanished.

Mick couldn't describe what had happened, because he genuinely didn't know. He just sensed that he'd discovered the antidote to his restlessness, the remedy to the you're-a-screwup mantra he'd been living with in one form or another all his life. The noise in his head had stopped, and he'd been content to simply hold a hammer, do the work and be with her. Selfishly, he hoped that whatever had put Mason under the weather would keep him there for a while so that Mick could continue to work with her on his own. Greedy? Yes. But he couldn't help himself.

"All right," Sarah Jane said, drawing his attention back to her. She straightened and cleared her throat. "Let's begin your official tour. You've seen the town square, of course—the hot spot for all of Monarch Grove's social activities—but there's a little bit of interesting history here I can share." She pointed to the gazebo in the middle of the grassy lawn. "For instance, that pretty piece of architecture was donated to our city by Mr. and Mrs. Homer Jenkins—"

Mick nodded, though he hardly found that "interesting."

"—on the condition that their cremated ashes be placed inside the urn built into the middle of the floor upon their passing."

Mick swiveled to look at her, and felt his eyes widen. "Seriously?"

"Seriously. They've always been at the center of the social scene and don't see any reason that should change after they're—" her lips twitched "—dead."

"That's not interesting, Sarah Jane," Mick said, feeling a laugh bubble up his throat. "That's just plain weird."

"Oh, no," she insisted. "We've got another stop before we get to weird. This is just odd."

"Semantics," he teased, settling more comfortably into his seat. His gaze slid to her once more, to the soft smile playing over her lips and the single strand of long hair curling around her breast. He liked the blouse, Mick thought. Scoop necked, sleeveless. It showcased the barest hint of cleavage and her toned, tanned arms, and put him in mind of Daisy Duke.

Particularly the shorts, he decided, sucking a slow breath through his teeth as his eyes feasted on the stretch of bare leg next to him. He let them roam over her thigh, past her knee, down her shapely calf. And there, right above her ankle, his gaze stopped short, and he felt a smile touch his lips. *Well, I'll be damned.* She had a tat. A blackberry vine, complete with flowers and berries, twined around her ankle and wound its way over the top of her foot.

Sarah Jane looked up and saw him smiling. "What are you grinning about?" she asked suspiciously.

"Your tattoo. I don't think I've ever seen one quite like that."

"Well, they are supposed to be original to their owners, right?"

"I suppose. Why a blackberry vine?"

She shrugged. "I just like them," she said, though the answer seemed a bit evasive. She swallowed. "My mother always loved them, particularly the wild ones. We used to spend hours in the summer picking berries. She'd make jams and jellies and cobblers." Sarah Jane made a humming noise in her throat, as though remembering the taste. "It's her recipe I enter into the fried-pie contest every year."

Ah, Mick thought, inclining his head. *There's the significance.* That small wild berry represented happy memories of her mother, ones that, like her life, were short-lived and bittersweet.

"I can't wait to try that pie," he said, surprised to realize just how much he meant it.

She chuckled. "I hope it lives up to the hype. What about you?" she asked. "Have you got a tattoo?"

"I do," he admitted, but didn't elaborate, instinctively knowing it would drive her nuts.

"Well?" she prodded.

Mick shot her a slow smile and had the privilege of watching her breath catch in her throat. "I'll tell you just like I told Perv—I don't know you well enough." He paused and purposely let his gaze drop to her mouth and linger. "Yet."

HER EVIL PLAN WAS WORKING, Sarah Jane thought as she released a shallow, shuddering breath. That "yet" hung like a promise between them, simultaneously raising her heart rate and the temperature inside the cab of her truck.

Mick finally stopped staring at her mouth, which had begun to water, and his blue eyes tangled with hers once more. "So we've seen odd and have one more stop to make before we get to weird. Where are we going now?"

"Back by the B and B," she said. She pulled up to the curb and stared at the old Victorian mansion. "It's got a unique history, as well."

He slid her a suspicious glance. "Unique?"

"Well, it's haunted. I'd say that's pretty damned unique."

Mick swore under his breath. "Are you shittin' me?"

Sarah Jane chuckled at his slightly horrified tone. "No, I'm not. The house was built by Byron Monarch, who founded our little town. Byron was an astute businessman, a butterfly aficionado, due to his last name, which is why there are butterflies worked into the architecture all over town, and—" she sighed heavily "—he was flamingly gay. If Clara, Tina and various other people who have stayed at the B and B are to be believed, old Byron is still there, occasionally copping a feel of unsuspecting male guests."

A choked laugh broke up in Mick's throat. "A gay ghost who sexually harasses the guests?"

Sarah Jane cocked her head and lifted her shoulders in a helpless shrug. "I'm only repeating what I've heard. I personally have no experience with Byron, but he's legendary in our little town. Clara actually enjoys that he's there, saying it gives the B and B a marketing edge. She's got a whole section of her Web site dedicated to Byron sightings. Has anything out of the ordinary happened to you?" Sarah Jane asked, pushing him a little further.

An odd look passed over his face, then he blinked. "No."

She chewed the inside of her cheek, not at all convinced. "Well, Clara's trying to get one of those paranormal programs to do a documentary on the B and B—she says it'll be good for business. So if you do experience anything odd, be sure and let her know."

He darted her a wry look. "You mean if I feel a cold hand grab my ass, or something like that?"

Sarah Jane grinned. "Exactly. A cold hand on your ass would definitely qualify. Actually, the most common thing that's been reported is a strong scent of aftershave in the air when none has been used."

Mick had that odd look again. "I'll be sure and let her know."

Sarah Jane pulled away from the curb and tooled around town, living up to her role as official tour guide by showcasing more points of interest. "That's Mabel's," she said. "Best place in Monarch Grove to get a true Southern meal, but don't you ever tell Clara I said that. Mabel and Clara have got a food feud going on that makes the Hatfields and McCoys look like amateurs." She chuckled darkly. "And Mabel might be an old-fashioned name, but she's far from ancient. She teaches feng shui and beginning computer classes at the senior center, and holds a black belt in karate." Sarah Jane pointed to a little crooked building across the street. "There's Buck's Barbershop. He's been in business since he was sixteen. He's seventy-five, still has a steady hand and still uses a straightedge razor to complete a shave."

Smiling, Mick nodded. "Sounds like my kind of man."

She felt her lips twitch. "You use a straightedge razor to shave?"

"No," he admitted, pushing a hand through those messy chocolate waves. "I use disposable. But you have to admire a man who still kicks it old school, right?"

"This is a small town, Mick. Old school around here is pretty much the *only* school."

"I wouldn't say that," he argued. "Clara's got Wi-Fi."

Sarah Jane nodded and chewed the inside of her cheek. "You're right. She does. But only because it's almost impossible for her to keep up with celebrity gossip otherwise."

He quirked a brow. "Clara's addicted to celebrity gossip?"

"And she's been known to surf a little porn."

Mick stared at her incredulously. "You're yanking my chain."

Smiling, Sarah Jane shook her head. "Mason had to fix her computer and found a little girl-on-girl action on there."

His eyes widened farther. "So she's…"

"Either that or she stumbled on it by mistake. She's never married, though—to my knowledge, never even dated—so my bet is on the former."

"Well, I'll be damned," Mick said, turning to watch the passing landscape as they drove out of town. "So much for small towns being boring."

"And you thought all we had to offer was the Fried Pie Festival."

He frowned. "When is that, exactly?"

"It kicks off next Friday afternoon."

"In the town square, right?"

"Right. Booths will be set up on Thursday. It's quite a spectacle, actually."

"How so?"

Sarah Jane merely grinned. "You'll see. Okay," she said. "I've shown you interesting and odd. Are you ready for weird?"

Mick gave his head a small shake, and an endearingly sexy smile tugged at the corner of his lips. Something about that half grin more than turned her on—it caused an odd fluttering in her chest. "I don't know," he said. "Am I?"

She gestured past his shoulder. "Look there."

A surprised snicker erupted from his throat. "A *teepee?* In *Georgia?*"

"That's not just any teepee," Sarah Jane explained. She turned into the long driveway that led out to Carl's new abode. "It's an authentic, hand-painted teepee, created in the Sioux style." Sarah Jane smiled. "Squatting Buck will be happy to tell you all about it."

"Has he always lived in a teepee?"

"Er, no. That's the funny part. Carl lived in a 1960s brick rancher complete with a deck and carport right up until he made a fateful trip to the Great Smoky Mountains last fall and discovered the Indian portion of his mostly German heritage." She smiled. "He found himself at a First Nations reserve, and he settled in for a while, learning from them. He was even given an Indian name by the elders, although personally, I think they did it as a bit of a joke. Anyway, after a few months, he returned home wearing lots of feathers, bones and turquoise, and decided to 'live off the land, as his ancestors had.'"

Mick grunted, seemingly amazed.

"Unfortunately, his marriage didn't survive the regression. He and Gladys parted ways a few months ago. She kept the house and furnishings and Carl took their generator, all their camping supplies and the truck."

Wearing a bewildered you're-bullshitting-me smile, Mick turned to look at her. "Does Squatting Buck have a job?"

Sarah Jane nodded. "He does. He's the bank manager at our local savings and loan."

Mick snorted. "I don't know whether to be impressed or appalled."

She shifted into Park and grabbed the jar of preserves she'd brought for Carl. "A gift for his time," she explained at Mick's raised brow.

He inclined his head: "One question. Where does he bathe?"

"He works out at the gym every morning and showers there."

Mick passed a hand over his face. "I've heard of going green, but this…this is unbelievable."

"I thought we agreed that it's weird?"

Mick whistled low under his breath when Carl emerged from the teepee wearing only a loincloth. A bone-and-turquoise choker encircled his neck and a feather dangled from a short stubby braid in his ever-lengthening light blond hair. "Oh, yeah, we've definitely arrived at weird."

Sarah Jane slid out of the truck and called a greeting to Carl. "Good evening, Squatting Buck. How're you doing?"

"Blessed with a cool breeze, Warrior Bleeding Heart," Carl replied, wrapping her in a warm, slightly sweaty hug.

"I hope you don't mind," she said, handing him the preserves, "but I brought a friend along with me."

"Certainly not," Carl told her. Morphing smoothly into banker mode, he extended his hand. "Nice to meet you, young man. Any friend of Sarah Jane's is a friend of mine."

"Mick Chivers," he said, shaking Carl's hand. He glanced at the teepee. "This is an interesting setup you've got here."

"Hardly conventional, I know, but intensely freeing. Popular thought is that I'm having a midlife crisis or going a little crazy, but I ignore the gossip. I've got no mortgage, no bills. It's just me and my thoughts, and a better ability to listen to the land."

Sarah Jane wondered how he heard it over the Braves baseball game blaring from the radio inside, but she wisely kept that thought to herself.

Carl gestured toward his leather-and-canvas home. "Would you like to see inside? It's quite remarkable, actually."

Mick nodded, seemingly intrigued. "If you're sure it's not an inconvenience."

"Not at all, not at all," Carl told him. "Come on in."

"Warrior Bleeding Heart?" Mick asked under his breath as they ventured inside the teepee.

Dammit, Sarah Jane thought. She'd hoped he'd missed that. "It's not an official Indian name like Carl's—tribal elders bestow those, and it's actually a great honor to be given one," she explained. "But Carl thinks it fits, and I appreciate the sentiment."

His voice dropped low. "Are you a warrior, Sarah Jane?"

She felt a wry smile curl her lips. "I think that's just a nice way of saying I've got a nasty temper."

Mick turned and studied her intently, and the unexpected scrutiny made her queasy. She saw admiration and respect, longing and the briefest shadow of what looked curiously like regret in those twin blue pools. He slid the pad of his thumb along her chin, snatching the breath from her lungs. "Depends on who that temper is directed at and for what reason, doesn't it, Warrior Bleeding Heart?" And with that parting comment, he ducked inside.

For the first time in her life, Sarah Jane wished she had some sort of clairvoyant talent. Because she'd give anything to know just exactly what was going through Mick's mind at that moment.

7

"SHOULD I BE OFFENDED that he didn't give me an Indian name?" Mick asked as they pulled out of Carl's driveway.

Though he couldn't argue with the "weird" assessment, he also had to admit he'd come away with a bit of respect for the guy. Carl had voluntarily made a huge change in his life and had fully embraced it, the good and the bad. Mick could honestly say he didn't know anybody who would willingly give up running water—most notably a toilet—electricity and climate control.

In the interest of his health, Carl did have a small dorm-size refrigerator and a hot plate, but most of his meals were cooked outside over an open flame. That part of Squatting Buck's existence really appealed to the lone caveman gene still lurking in Mick's domesticated DNA, but he imagined he'd grow weary of it pretty damn quick. Carl had already survived one winter out here—quite comfortably, he'd said—and seemed to be doing fine during this broiling summer.

"No, you shouldn't be offended. It's not like he tosses names out to every person he meets," she teased.

Mick grinned. "Are you trying to say that Carl thinks you're special?"

Actually, it was painfully obvious that Carl thought a lot of Sarah Jane. He'd asked her about her work and her animals, and made a point to tell her to let him know if she ever needed anything. He'd also mentioned, as covertly as possible, that her stepmother had made a sizable withdrawal for a down payment on a vacation home. The worry that had wrinkled Sarah Jane's brow had been echoed in Mick's chest, but the determined chew-nails-and-spit-bullets look immediately following made him want to chuckle with pride. Why?

Who the hell knew? And at this point he was tired of trying to make sense of his motivation.

Sarah Jane Walker was something else. Her heart, spirit, sense of humor and work ethic were an amazing combination, one he found increasingly hard to resist. Then there was the whole matter of her making him want to back her up against a wall and take her until her eyes rolled back in her head. Then take her again until his did.

This driving need, this utter desperation and increasing lack of control were something so new, so unique and so completely foreign to him. Mick felt himself slowly sinking into a pit of sexual hell where she was his only hope for survival. He couldn't look at her without feeling it, an increasingly insistent pull that affected both his groin and, more disturbingly, a soft spot in his chest.

Frankly, Mick didn't have any idea how much money she stood to inherit, though he probably should make it a point to find out. At any rate, he knew it had to be a pretty hefty nest egg; otherwise, Chastity could hardly afford to pay for their services, nor would she have gone to the trouble to hire Ranger Security to keep Sarah Jane from finding the will. He'd seen the agreement, been told his cut and knew the surveillance didn't come cheap.

Furthermore, if Sarah Jane had a prayer of keeping the remainder for herself or getting any of the other money back, she'd better act fast. Otherwise, he had a sneaking suspicion there wouldn't be anything left. Maybe that had been part of her stepmother's plan, as well, Mick thought, his senses going on point. Maybe Chastity hadn't been happy with her part and had every intention of depleting the accounts before Sarah Jane could find and probate the will.

"Can I help it if I'm special?" Sarah Jane asked, batting her lashes at him playfully, dragging his thoughts back to the conversation at hand.

He grunted, amused. "No more than you can help being full of shit, I guess."

"Hey," she said, feigning outrage. "My Indian name is Warrior Bleeding Heart, not Princess Full of Shit." Her speculative eyes raked over him, sizing him up, and his dick literally stood to attention, as though she'd stroked him with more than her gaze. "You definitely need an Indian name," she said. "And before you leave town, I'm going to come up with one for you."

So long as it wasn't Little Limp Dick, he wouldn't object. He shrugged. "Knock yourself out, sweetheart. I don't mind." He paused. "How did Carl wind up with Squatting Buck? It's a bit..." He struggled to find the right word.

"Ignoble," Sarah Jane suggested.

Mick grinned. "That would be it, yes. I wanted to ask, but wasn't sure if it would be polite. My Indian etiquette is pretty nonexistent."

"I don't think he would have had a problem with it. Carl's last name is Hirsh, which is German for 'buck.' He wanted something that would reflect that heritage, as well."

Mick nodded thoughtfully. "Makes sense. But why 'Squatting'? Why not 'Running' or 'Walking' or, hell, even 'Sitting'? Something a bit more dignified. Do bucks even squat?" he wondered aloud, frowning. Honestly, he'd never watched a deer do his business, but couldn't imagine one squatting to get the job done.

Sarah Jane shrugged. "To tell you the truth, I don't know why the tribal elders chose 'Squatting,' but I'm sure it has some sort of significance."

Mick grimaced. "I think I would have asked for another one."

Another strangled laugh emerged from her throat. "I'm not up on Indian etiquette, either, but I don't b-believe that's an o-option."

He paused and turned to look at her. "You're laughing at me."

"Sorry," she said, her voice cracking with suppressed amusement. "I can't seem to help myself." She cleared her throat. "So I take it you don't want the word *squatting* to be any part of the Indian name I give you?"

His lips twitched and he nodded. "That would be an excellent assumption."

Still smiling, Sarah Jane again made that humming noise in her throat. The late evening sunshine was spreading out in an orange, pink and purple display across the horizon. Rather than using the AC, she'd powered down her window, causing her loose hair to whirl around her face, occasionally clinging to her eyelashes and mouth. She'd abandoned the sunglasses and looked relaxed and content, at peace with her world.

Curiously, though he definitely wasn't at peace with his *own* world, Mick felt an odd kind of serenity just being with her. He'd noticed it this afternoon, after he'd returned from taking Mason home. There'd been the two of them in that old house, music playing from her portable radio, dust motes dancing through the hot summer air....

Despite her initial protest, he'd set his camera aside and picked up a hammer and, for the first time since the Carson Wells incident, he'd felt more alive—more *himself*—than he had in months. Whether it was her company or the work or a combination of both, he couldn't be sure.

He just knew that it had felt...right.

Though he hated that Mason was sick, Mick wouldn't mind in the least if the man didn't show up for work tomorrow. Or the next day. Or the next. He selfishly wanted to explore this newfound well-being, and he could hardly do that if Mason was there.

Furthermore, though it was the height of idiocy, Mick wanted to be alone with Sarah Jane. He wanted the opportunity to get to know her better. And not just in the physical sense, although that was an ever-present urge, chugging through his veins and swirling in his loins. He literally itched to touch her skin, to feel the silken softness of her cheek against the palm of his hand, to taste her mouth and her neck and the delicate tips of her breasts.

Though he would like to blame this supernatural attraction on the fact that she was supposed to be off-limits—and even recognized that it no doubt added to her appeal on his hell-raiser scale—Mick knew there was more to it than that. He was a man, after all, and no stranger to his baser needs. He'd been attracted to lots of women before and, frankly, had had most of them. He'd always been goal oriented, and when he set his mind on something—or *someone*—he typically developed tunnel vision and single-mindedly worked away until he'd accomplished his objective. That focused tenacity had ultimately been his downfall, Mick thought, swallowing.

At any rate, whatever this was with Sarah Jane—this unshakable, driving, had-to-have-her need—he knew it was more than just regular, old garden-variety lust.

It was more.

It involved curiosity and intrigue and affection and, God help him, *feelings.*

He couldn't name them, of course, and wouldn't if he could. But he couldn't deny them all the same…which was going to make ignoring them all the more difficult.

Sarah Jane hung a left onto a long, tree-lined drive—the very one he'd watched her disappear down yesterday evening—plunging the truck into cool semi-darkness. He peered out the window, but couldn't see anything for all the trees.

He lifted a brow. "Where are we going?"

She smiled. "To my dream house," she said. "I was sick over the fate of the Milton Plantation, but if this one were to go the same way…" Her voice trailed off and she released a small sigh as a break in the trees finally revealed a beautiful old house sitting atop a knoll in the distance.

Mick gave a low whistle, instantly struck by the beauty and setting. "Wow."

And "wow" was an understatement. The two-story house sported large columns and a double verandah, and notably showcased a pretty stained-glass angel in an oval window on the second floor. An occasional black shutter hung next to one of the multipaned windows, giving a hint of what the place might have looked like in its heyday.

Sarah Jane pulled to a stop, turned off the ignition and opened her door. "Come on, we'll have to hurry. The light's fading."

Mick exited the vehicle, as well, and, taking it all in, followed her around to the back, where an unlocked door hung from its hinges. "Are we trespassing?"

She shot him a look over her shoulder and snorted. "As if you'd care if we were...."

Mick smiled, conceding the point.

"Like so many houses of this era, the kitchen was separate, and all that's left of it is the foundation," she said. She carefully opened the door and gingerly stepped inside, then gestured to the windows on her left. "It's shaped like a horseshoe, so all of the rooms open onto the courtyard."

Mick nodded, impressed.

"Were I to renovate this house, this room would have to be the kitchen." She walked into the next one. "And here's the dining room, of course."

"Makes sense." Enchanted, he stuffed his hands into

his pockets and strolled along in her wake. The next room was bigger and grander, with a giant fireplace at one end.

"Family room."

Mick looked up. "What are these? Ten-foot ceilings?"

"Twelve." She wandered over to a front window and stared out at the landscape. "There isn't a bad view in the place, Mick. I love this little hill, the trees marching along the driveway. It's peaceful and elegant...and lonely." She looked over at him and smiled a bit uncomfortably. "You think I'm a nut, don't you?"

He rubbed the back of his neck. "Not at all. You've spent so much time working on old places like this, I'd be surprised if you didn't feel some sort of connection."

"It's stronger here," she admitted. "It has been even when I was a kid, coming out here to make the odd repair with my father. I've even done a little research, wondering if perhaps any of my family ever worked here."

Why not *lived* here? Mick mused. Seemingly following his thought process, Sarah Jane smiled wryly. "My heritage is strictly working class. My ancestors could never have afforded anything like this."

He bit the inside of his cheek. "So have you found anything?"

She shook her head, causing a lock of hair to shift tantalizingly over her breast. "Not yet. But I can't deny the feeling that there's something here." She shrugged. "I'm just going to have to keep looking, I guess."

And she would, Mick knew, because it was important to her. Another admirable trait to add to his growing list of many. Mick wandered into the foyer, keen to inspect the rest of the house before it grew too dark. A beautiful staircase clung to the wall to the left, paused at a large landing, where it made an abrupt turn and continued upward.

Sarah Jane joined him. "Beautiful architecture, isn't it?"

"Amazing," he agreed.

"And just think. All of this was done before the age of the power saw, nail gun and pneumatic tools. By hand. When it took time and attention to detail. No prefab work." Her eyes glittered with a hint of challenge. "Do you want to go upstairs?"

Mick peered into the next room. "What about the rest?"

Sarah Jane carefully put a foot on the first tread. "It's a mirror image of what you just saw. Three more rooms, all open to the courtyard, which would house my pool, of course." She took another step. "Come on. I've done this so many times I know which steps are sound and which ones aren't."

"For your weight," he said. "But what about mine?"

"It'll hold. And it's worth it," she promised. "Just watch where I go and give me a couple steps head start."

If he'd been any other guy, he would have chastised her for taking chances—old house plus rotten wood plus staircase equaled potential disaster. But he wasn't any other guy, he was The Hell-raiser. And she wasn't just any other girl. She was a woman who wasn't afraid of hard work, who wasn't afraid to throw a punch and who wasn't afraid to trespass on private property.

In fact, at the moment, he could honestly believe that she wasn't afraid of anything. Envy and respect grabbed hold of his insides and twisted. Oh, to have that sort of confidence again, Mick thought, following her up the stairs. To have that sort of assurance, that faith in one's ability.

Still, if he had any sense at all, he'd be afraid of *her*. Because, God help him, Sarah Jane Walker, if she put her mind to it, could undoubtedly bring him to his knees.

And in exchange, he'd bring her to hers, but not in the same sense, unfortunately. Like everything else he'd been involved with in recent memory, he would infect her with his bad mojo and turn her life into a steaming pile that mirrored his own. Honestly, right now his world was so messed up he didn't have any business being anywhere near her. She was perfect—in every way that he could see—and despite the issue with the will and inheritance, she seemed happy. He didn't want to screw that up for her. And becoming emotionally involved would do it faster than Clara's resident ghost could say boo.

Mick needed to alert Huck to the change in status of this case, then get the hell out of here before he did something completely stupid. Like kiss her.

And more.

Having reached the landing, she stood at the window overlooking the vast landscape. Seeing her silhouetted against the sunset, the wistfulness in her eyes and the hint of pleasure in the curve of her mouth, was almost his undoing. He felt that ball of unnamed emotion expand in his chest, almost choking him.

Mick silently released a shaky breath, then sidled in beside her, purposely invading her space because he simply couldn't stay away. Couldn't help himself. She was the only bright spot in his otherwise dismal world, and he was drawn to her like the proverbial moth to a flame. He caught the scent of her perfume—a combination of apples and warmth—and he breathed her in, savoring the smell. "You were right," he murmured.

"I usually am, but about what, specifically?"

A chuckle erupted from his throat and he shook his head. "You don't have a modest bone in your body, do you?"

"I do," she said, turning to look at him. A hint of mischief shone in her eyes, and something else...something less easily defined. "But it's very small."

Unable to help himself, he laughed again. "I meant you were right about the view. It's gorgeous. And I love the stained glass." He paused, moved by the house and its surroundings more than he could have imagined.

A faint grin, rife with a hint of embarrassment, shaped her lips. "That's my wishing angel," she said, pointing to a figure etched in the stained glass. "When I was a little girl, I used to make wishes on it, fancying that she could hear me and would someday honor my requests."

Mick felt his lips twitch. "What did you wish for?"

"Oh, the usual stuff. The occasional good grade, a new bike, for Kirk Cameron to come into town and fall instantly in love with me."

Mick chuckled. "Kirk Cameron?"

"Hey, don't judge," she admonished. "Kirk was hot." She sighed, remembering. "But mostly I just wished I could live here. This is a *great* house."

It was. The dilapidated Milton Plantation was sad, but seeing this place fall to ruin was far worse. The structure wasn't past the point of no return, but was getting there quickly. "What's the name of this place?" Mick asked. "Who owns it? Why have they let it sink into disrepair?"

"Officially, it's named Ponder Hill." She hesitated, then blew out an uneasy breath. "Unofficially, it's called The Widow-maker."

Mick felt a smile tug at the corner of his mouth. "I think Ponder Hill is more aesthetically pleasing, but for the sake of argument, *why* is it called The Widow-maker?"

"Because Imogene Childress has buried three husbands who basically worked themselves to death keeping the place up. She has no heirs, is in her nineties and refuses to sell it." Sarah Jane tucked a strand of hair behind the delicate shell of her ear. "She hopes the whole thing falls to rack and ruin so that it doesn't 'claim the life of another good man.'" Sarah Jane delivered the last in a theatrical, quavery voice that would have done Broadway proud.

Mick grunted. "Sounds like Imogene has a flair for the dramatic."

"Whether she does or she doesn't, it's hers, and I haven't been the only one who's tried to persuade her to sell. She absolutely refuses."

"So…what? Did her husbands fall off the roof making repairs? Tumble down the stairs?"

Humor sparkled in Sarah Jane's eyes. "Husband number one had a heart attack at the card table, number two suffered a stroke in his sleep and number three died of cancer." She shrugged helplessly. "Did the house kill them? No. But you'll never convince her of that." Sarah Jane looked at the ever-darkening sky. "We'd better get going. It's getting late."

Though he found himself reluctant to leave, Mick nodded and started back down the stairs.

"Wait," she said. "I should go first."

"Don't worry," he told her. "I know the way back down."

She smiled, considering him. "You're sure? It's a little tricky."

He'd survived military school, some of the most rigorous military training in the world, enemy fire and countless stunts resulting in the occasional broken bone, but never wounded pride. Oh, yeah. He thought he could handle it.

What he couldn't handle, he was beginning to realize, was *her*.

"SO, HAVE YOU COME UP with it yet?" Mick asked, as Sarah Jane pulled back into her driveway. While Blinken was AWOL, Winken and Nod sat in the front window, and a flutter of curtains told her the dogs were nosing the gauzy fabric aside, evidently recognizing the sound of her truck. A blanket of warmth settled over her as she watched her furry family eagerly, as always, await her return.

But for the first time in her life, Sarah Jane was nervous about coming home. Mick was about to walk her to her door, and the anxiety of whether or not that first kiss—the one she wanted so desperately she'd forgone the onion rings at Mabel's—was going to happen was shredding her nerves like a wood chipper stuck on High.

"Have I come up with what yet?" she asked, trying valiantly to stay tuned to the conversation.

The smile that curved his beautiful lips was so sexy and knowing, her stomach actually gave a little roll. "My Indian name," he reminded her.

That had quickly turned into a running joke, she mused, remembering the "Virile Badass" suggestion he'd tossed out over dinner. Quite frankly, she thought "Virile Badass" suited him perfectly, and the more time she spent with him, the more apt the moniker seemed.

He was certainly both. Still…

"How many times do I have to tell you," she said, "that when I think of one I'll let you know? The name has to be organic, not dragged from the shadow of your enormous ego."

Mick closed the truck door and followed her up onto her porch. Her gurgling koi pond mingled with the other night noises, creating a natural soundtrack to her ever-growing nervousness and off-the-charts attraction. It was insanity to want someone so much. Beyond rational thought.

"Enormous ego?" He scoffed, feigning offense. "Where on earth did you get the idea that I have an enormous ego?"

Her hands trembling, Sarah Jane fished her house key out of her small purse, but hesitated before slipping it into the lock. She felt a wry smile tilt her lips as she turned to face him, then almost jumped when she realized he was much closer than she'd thought.

She was *so* definitely getting kissed tonight, she decided, feeling a wicked thrill whip through her midsection. She resisted the urge to do a screaming little happy dance and felt a burst of anticipation coursing through her blood.

"Where would I get the idea that you've got an enormous ego?" Smiling, she chewed the inside of her cheek. "Well, let's review a few of your suggestions tonight, shall we?"

Mick's twinkling blue gaze dropped to her lips, darkened, then found hers once more. "If you insist," he murmured.

Oy. Those blue flame eyes coupled with that sexy, endearing mouth were going to be her downfall.

With any luck, right onto a mattress.

Clearly, she'd lost her mind. Hadn't she decided he was trouble? That he had more issues than she could take on? That he'd never stay here? Didn't she know where all of this would lead?

Yes, she did. The problem was...she didn't care. She just wanted him. Every wonderful, magnificently pro-portioned inch of him.

"I, uh, I do," Sarah Jane said. "Let's see... We've covered Virile Badass. Then there was Brilliant Badass and Handsome Badass." She cocked her head to the side. "I'm recognizing a theme here. You seem to be obsessed with being a badass."

Mick laughed softly, the sound curiously intimate between them. "I'd hardly want to be a pansy ass, would I?"

An unladylike grunt rose in her throat and she rolled her eyes. "I don't think anyone would ever mistake you for that."

"You, either," he said, in what was possibly the best compliment anyone had ever paid her. Whether he was simply that insightful or her expectations were just too low, who could say? All Sarah Jane knew, as she blushed with pleasure from the inside out, was that Mick Chivers affected her on a level she'd never experienced and instinctively knew would never be duplicated.

Mick's gaze tangled with hers, seemingly drawing her closer. At that very moment she hovered on the edge of an existence that was about to be permanently altered. Life as she knew it was a mere few seconds away from irreparable change.

And for better or worse, she didn't care. She just wanted to taste him. She had to.

He cupped her cheek, the gesture simultaneously sexy and affectionate, pulling a soft sigh from between her lips...

"Sarah Jane," he said huskily, his mouth a hairsbreadth from her own.

"Um-hmm." Talking wasn't an option. She could feel his breath, smell him, even. Dark, dangerous, musky and man all rolled into one drugging aroma that made her lids grow heavy and her sex ache. Her nipples tingled and her knees weakened, making her lean closer to him.

"Can I kiss you?"

His asking was quaint and old-fashioned, and while she would have never associated those qualities with this eternal bad boy, to her surprise, they actually fit, making the moment all the more special.

Touched, she smiled against his lips. "Not if I kiss you first," she whispered, then pushed her hands into his hair and drew him down to her.

Everything inside her simultaneously stilled and erupted at the first brush of his lips across hers. Her skin prickled, her hair stood on end and a wave of gooseflesh engulfed every inch of her body, including parts she hadn't thought could shiver. The anticipation of a first kiss was one of life's great pleasures, one of the few things that could never be duplicated. Scores of odes and sonnets had been written about the phenomenon of that first mating of the mouths, that intimate mimicry of another much anticipated act. Sarah Jane Walker had been the recipient of many first kisses, some of them eager, some of them stolen, some of them to simply end a date.

But absolutely nothing in her experience had ever compared to *this* first kiss.

It was heartbreakingly perfect, desperate and dangerous, the disease and the cure. It was as though every moment up until this point had simply been a precursor to this event. If her brain had been anything but mush, she would have been absolutely terrified.

As it was…she just wanted more.

Mick's lips were surprisingly soft, but warm and pliant and every bit as magnificent as she'd imagined. A deep groan erupted from his chest as he drew her closer, one strong arm banding around her waist, while his other hand slipped past her jaw, into her hair, cupping her head. Deliberate fingers kneaded her scalp as his tongue slid against hers, a mind-numbingly wonderful combination of sensations that made her stomach flutter and her pulse sing. She sighed in pleasure, in relief because she'd wanted this so desperately. Meanwhile, another sort of urgency had taken hold.

She felt her nipples pebble behind the flimsy fabric of her bra, and a rush of warmth pooled in her core. Her blood surged hotly through her veins, making her feel both anxious and languid at the same time.

Mick suckled her tongue, making her bones melt

and her body sag against him. The hard ridge of his arousal nudged impatiently at her belly, causing another wicked thrill to swirl through her middle.

Hot, hard, male.

It had been *so* long and he was *so* perfect. She resisted the urge to whimper as she kissed him more deeply, mapping his body with her hands. Muscles bunched beneath her fingers, warm and supple. She inhaled his scent as she fed at his mouth, growing more hungry and needy by the second.

Thankfully, Mick was, too.

She could feel the tension hovering within him, could taste it on her tongue, heard it in the soft groans of pleasure bubbling up his throat. His hands slid slowly down her back, as though memorizing every vertebra, then settled warmly over her bottom and squeezed. That small amount of pressure literally made the breath leave her lungs. It was strangely possessive, which should have pissed her off, but instead made her moronic heart skip a beat.

Sarah Jane pressed herself even more tightly against him, determined to eliminate the barest hint of separation. Mick responded by holding her closer, branding her with his masculine frame. He rocked against her belly once more and carefully backed her up against a porch pole, where he nipped at her earlobe and licked a path along her neck, tasting the pulse point and nuzzling her throat. Meanwhile his hands had left her bottom and were making a determined track back up her body, along her hip, up her side. She whimpered aloud this time, longing to feel the weight of her breast in his big, warm palm. To feel his mouth there, licking and tasting and suckling with those talented, sinfully made lips.

Heat rushed to her core and she squirmed desperately against him, aligning herself more firmly against the impossibly large ridge straining the front of his pants. She wiggled closer as his hand finally brushed the underside of her breast, gasping when the slight contact made her skin prickle in anticipation. *Higher,* she thought, her nipple drawing into a tight bud. *Oh, please, just a little—*

A police siren, followed by a catcall, abruptly cut through her foggy, lust-ridden thoughts, and she sprang back guiltily.

"It's a good thing you're on your porch, Sarah Jane, or I'd have to take you in for lewd and lascivious behavior," Chase called after he'd pulled up in his squad car.

Mortified, she felt her face flame. "Go away, Chase. Don't you have anything better to do?"

He nodded toward Mick. "Is this Mr. Gorgeous?"

Mick frowned, but humor danced in his heavy-lidded gaze, betraying a hint of masculine pride. "Mr. Gorgeous? Is that my Indian nickname?"

She chuckled. "No. Your Indian name won't have a 'mister' in it." *Goofball,* she thought, enjoying his pleased smile.

"Chase Collins," Chase called out to Mick. "Old friend of Sarah Jane's." He shook his head regretfully as though she was a poor testament to Southern hospitality. "She seems to have forgotten her manners."

Sarah Jane harrumphed. "My tax dollars at work," she grumbled.

"Mick Chivers, new friend of Sarah Jane's." He shot her a look. "And I *hope* I'm Mr. Gorgeous."

"You the photographer?" Chase asked conversationally, while Sarah Jane entertained thoughts of throttling him.

Mick nodded and his grin grew wider. "I am."

"Oh. Then you're Mr. Gorgeous." Evidently deciding his work here was done, Chase nodded and, smiling like the evil shit-stirring bastard he was, rode off into the night.

Mick's curiously hesitant gaze found Sarah Jane's and he rubbed the back of his neck. "So…what sort of friend is he, exactly?"

Jealous, was he? she wondered, inwardly blushing with pleasure. "The sort that gets on my nerves." Not the answer he was looking for, she knew, but…

Mick grunted. "That covers a lot of territory."

Sarah Jane decided to take pity on him. "I've known Chase since kindergarten," she said. "Other than a brief 'Do-you-love-me? Check-yes-or-no' flirtation in second grade—where our romance came to a tragic end on the playground after I beat him in the fifty-yard dash—we've been nothing but friends ever since."

Mick chuckled, the deep sound resonating through her. "Couldn't stand losing to a girl, eh?"

She sighed dramatically. "It's been a recurring problem, I'm afraid. I don't like to lose and don't see any point in doing it simply to inflate some boy's pride. Ya'll are the ones with balls," she said, rolling her eyes. "Use them, for pity's sake."

Another chuckle sounded in Mick's throat, quickly morphing into a belly laugh. "Interesting ph-philosophy. And refreshingly blunt. You're something else, Sarah Jane," he said, seemingly impressed. "Truly unique."

Sarah Jane nodded, suddenly feeling a bit awkward. "Thank you. I like to think so."

His amused gaze found hers once more and the world again shrank into a more intimate focus. "I've had a good time tonight." His voice was low and sincere, wrapping about her like an embrace. "Thank you for showing me around."

Sarah Jane nodded again, suddenly feeling a bit awkward. "You're welcome."

"I should probably get going. I'd hate for you to be arrested for lewd and lascivious behavior on my account."

For the teeniest second, she considered pointing out that she could hardly get arrested for those things if she invited him in, but ultimately decided he was right. Though her body begged to differ, her mind had honed in on some long-forgotten sense of self-preservation, and wasn't yet ready to surrender.

She pursed her lips, playing along. "You're right, of course. I know Tina is growing weary of bailing me out of jail."

He fingered a petunia petal. "Happens that often, does it?"

"Nah," she said. "Just often enough to keep everybody on their toes."

His wicked laugh came again, the one that made her want to crawl inside him and never come out. "I can certainly see where you do that." He leaned forward and pressed a lingering kiss on her cheek. "Good night, Sarah Jane. I'll see you in the morning."

From inside the house, Sarah Jane heard her phone ring, which thankfully prevented her from standing on her porch and watching him drive away like a love-struck teenager.

As for her really keeping people on their toes, she sincerely doubted it, and couldn't imagine *anyone* keeping Mick Chivers on his. Utterly laughable.

But she knew that *hers* had been curled for the better part of the evening.

8

MICK WATCHED SARAH JANE dart into the house to catch her ringing phone, and wished like hell he could follow her. Only he wouldn't have let her answer it, instead insisting they take up right where Chase Collins had, quite irritatingly, interrupted.

Which, on the grand scale of Stupid Things He'd Done in His Life, would probably rate right up there at the top, dethroning the headmaster's daughter—on the man's office desk, no less—and sending Carson Wells over that ill-fated ridge when, as team leader, if anyone was going to take that chance, it should have been him. Mick had been certain—or as certain as he could be with the intel he'd been given—that the route was safe.

It hadn't been.

He swallowed.

At any rate, sleeping with Sarah Jane was more than beyond the height of idiocy, it was just plain wrong. He was here under false pretenses, and given what he'd gleaned from her tonight, he knew that he should call Huck to alert him to the change, and move on.

Simply put, he should leave.

As Payne had said, Ranger Security wouldn't be a party to anything illegal. And Chastity Walker using their services under false pretense to keep Sarah Jane from getting her rightful inheritance was definitely breaking some sort of law. He didn't know which one, precisely, but that hardly mattered.

Furthermore, in the event he slept with Sarah Jane and she somehow managed to find out who he really was—what he'd originally come here for—he didn't have a single doubt that she'd once again end up in jail, only it wouldn't be for lewd and lascivious behavior. It'd be for murder, because she'd undoubtedly kill him.

And he would deserve it.

This—being with her, kissing her, God help him, *liking* her—was all a mistake, but one he didn't know how to correct, and frankly, didn't want to.

Mick slid into his truck, cranked the engine and reluctantly pulled away from the curb. Rather than return to the B and B, he decided to drive around town for a little while. Knowing that a homosexual ghost was probably responsible for the weird hand-on-his-thigh feeling this morning when he'd awoken didn't exactly make him anxious to get back to Clara's, he thought darkly.

The town square was lit with pretty antique lampposts, illuminating older couples holding hands and chatting on park benches, kids playing in the fountain and the occasional Generation Xer walking a dog. Monarch Grove nightlife, Mick thought, feeling a smile steal over his lips.

Funny, he'd always been under the impression that small towns rolled up their sidewalks after dark. But the people of this little burg seemed more interested in talking to each other than watching reality TV. If he didn't know better, Mick would chalk up their habit to having no access to cable, but he knew that wasn't the case. Clara had a top-of-the-line satellite system providing hundreds of channels, some even in foreign languages, which accounted for the occasional Portuguese epithet he heard her mutter under her breath.

At any rate, this town along with its inhabitants—particularly one dark blond hellion with melting-toffee eyes—had turned every preconceived notion he'd had about it on its ear.

Though his grandfather had lived in Minot, Kentucky, most of his life, Mick couldn't help but think the older man would love it here. The last time he'd visited Charlie's old hometown, the place had all but died. The few businesses that hadn't folded when the larger chain stores were built out on the highway had abandoned the old town square and moved into strip malls to survive. Little by little, the new had eroded the old, and very few small businesses had survived the so-called "progress." Amazingly, Monarch Grove seemed to have been able to absorb the new without forgetting the old, a rare balance that took a special brand of people.

Mick snagged his cell phone from the holder at his waist and dialed his grandfather's number, ashamed that it had been more than three months since the last time he'd called. He'd been a wreck then, having just left the military. While he hadn't wanted to share the news with his dad, he couldn't *not* share the decision with Charlie.

His grandfather answered on the second ring. "Hello."

"Hey, Gramps. How's it going up there?"

"Same as it always is, Micky. Slow as molasses, boring as hell, but a body gets used to it." He paused. "How about you? Working your new job now?"

His body wouldn't get used to it, Mick thought, staring at the bustling activity around the square. His grandfather had always been so active, so full of purpose. "I am," he admitted. "I, er…I don't think it's going to work out," he said, giving voice to the niggling thought. Hell, he'd suspected when he'd taken the job that it wasn't for him, but Huck had been so sure it was the right thing to do. And Levi had seemed almost envious, which had somehow made Mick think that he was missing something they could see. Besides his own judgment had been shot to hell… He'd just said yes, thankful that anyone thought he was worth having.

Unfortunately, Mick wasn't sure what sort of work he was cut out for, but the security specialist field wasn't for him. It didn't fill the void in him—and though it pained him to admit it, even being a Ranger hadn't satisfied him the way he'd thought it would.

If there was any good thing that could come out of his recent screwup, it was the opportunity for him to finally find something he loved. Like Charlie had, Mick thought, envying his grandfather his purpose. Sarah Jane, too.

"Well, you're not a quitter and never have been—"

Though he knew that, hearing his grandfather say it was more important than he would have ever imagined. Mick swallowed tightly.

"—and if you ask me, I think you need to be working

with your hands. You're too much like me, Micky. Restless and miserable without a purpose. That's why carpentry always suited me so well. It was my outlet, so to speak. All that energy had to go somewhere, so I figured pouring it into a building was as good as any way to use it. Start with a blueprint, end up with a home, something to be proud of, tangible proof of labor. Then on to the next project." Though Mick couldn't see him, he could imagine his grandfather's shrug, the wisdom in his lined face. "At least, that's what I've always thought."

"I'll think about it, Gramps."

In truth, he had to admit he'd felt more content working with Sarah Jane today than he had in months, possibly longer. Breaking a sweat, feeling the weight of a hammer in his hands…it had all been very therapeutic. He'd completely lost track of time and had thoroughly enjoyed every minute. Of course, that could simply be a result of the company he'd been keeping, and not necessarily the work. Still, he didn't need to get too attached to either. He was at a crossroads at the moment, struggling to find his path, and dragging someone else along on his blind journey was hardly fair.

"Have you talked to your father? Told him about your recent occupational change?" his grandfather asked.

Mick hesitated. "Not yet. I haven't heard from him." And he hadn't called, either. Frankly, though he shouldn't give a damn, knowing the inevitable disappointment he'd hear in his father's voice had prevented Mick from making any effort to contact him. Becoming a Ranger was his only accomplishment that had ever impressed the man.

"Me, either," his grandfather said. "He and your mother must be on another one of their vacations. Probably off riding camels or looking for tigers or something."

Mick chuckled at the distaste in Charlie's voice. "Riding a camel might be fun."

"Men ride horses, boy. Not camels. Where are you, exactly?"

Mick rested his head against the back of his seat and smiled. "I'm in Monarch Grove, Georgia—Home of the Fried Pie Festival."

"You don't say?" Charlie replied, sounding genuinely interested. "I love fried pies. Haven't had a good one in years. Not since your grandmother passed away, anyway. Peach was always my favorite."

Mick felt his lips twitch. "I have it on good authority that blackberry is best."

"Oh, I bet that would be good. A fried-pie festival," he repeated, almost wistfully. "I can't say as I've ever been to one of those."

Mick couldn't say he'd ever *heard* of one, so his grandfather had him beat. "It starts next Friday afternoon, Gramps. You should come down. There isn't a room to be had in town, but I'll share mine with you." The spontaneous invitation caught him off guard, but it suddenly occurred to Mick just how much he meant it.

"Nah," his grandfather said, albeit reluctantly. "I've got too much air to breathe here. Might mess up the delicate balance of things if I'm not around doing my part."

Mick chuckled, mildly disappointed. "Just thought I'd offer."

"And I appreciate it. I'd love to see you. Speaking of which, when do you reckon you'll be in this neck of the woods? Anytime soon? Should I change the sheets in your room? Dust off the chessboard?"

Another reminiscent smile tugged at the corner of Mick's mouth. How many hours had he logged playing chess with Charlie? Hundreds, possibly thousands. "Soon, Gramps," he said, meaning it. In fact, when this was over, he'd go home. After all, his grandfather's old farmhouse was the closest thing to a home he'd ever known, the location of some of his best childhood memories. Were it not for his grandfather, Mick grimly suspected he wouldn't have had any at all.

Damn selfish parents, he thought. He hadn't been that bad. What had been so wrong with him that they hadn't wanted him? Weren't they supposed to love him unconditionally? Weren't they supposed to have had some sort of sentimental attachment to him? He'd read stories of mothers who performed heroic acts to save their children. His mother would, no doubt, be the exception to the rule.

She'd sure as hell never come to his rescue before. Not once, Mick thought bitterly.

He was an adult, old enough to reason and understand, mature enough to comprehend that he wasn't responsible for their emotional shortcomings. But there'd always been a small part of him that secretly thought if he was so flawed his own parents hadn't been able to invest a little love in him, then why would anyone else bother?

"I hope so, boy," his grandfather said, pulling him back to the conversation. "It's been too long."

Mick silently concurred, then listened to Charlie complain about his neighbor's fence and how he'd had to fix it for him, and how the portion sizes at the diner had gotten downright paltry. How nobody took pride in doing things right anymore, and that was the problem with the whole world, and America in particular. "Spoiled, the lot of them," Charlie muttered. Mick answered where appropriate and provided commentary for the better part of half an hour before he finally ended the call.

Still reluctant to go back to the B and B, he circled the square a couple more times, then parked a few houses down from Sarah Jane's, under the pretense of putting her under his new-and-improved form of surveillance—which involved keeping her out of Chastitiy's house, and thereby out of jail, until he could come up with a better plan—when truth be told, he just wanted to catch a glimpse of her.

Pathetic, Chivers. Utterly pathetic.

And yet he knew it was true. He couldn't deny that he'd been completely enchanted by her from the minute he'd looked at the blurry, out-of-focus picture. Sarah Jane Walker was the real deal. She was honest and forthright, hardworking and funny, loyal and loving. She could kiss like the very devil and would undoubtedly take that same skill and fervor into the bedroom. His dick jerked hard against his zipper, where it no doubt bore a permanent imprint after he'd spent the entire evening with her.

Mick honestly didn't think he'd ever enjoyed a woman's company more, and knew beyond a shadow of a doubt that he'd never been so affected by a mere kiss. He had always liked the taste of a woman against his tongue, eating those soft inhalations, the slide of feminine lips against his, the suckling of tongues, the mimicry of making love with the mouth. It was erotic and pleasurable, and in many respects, just as enjoyable as sex. Would every man agree with him? No, probably not, he decided, silently chuckling at the thought.

But from the moment he'd stolen his first kiss in second grade, he'd always been a huge fan. In his opinion, a man had a lot riding on that first kiss. If he was sloppy, or too eager or too lazy, he might as well forget making it to the next base. A kiss should enflame, not be a hasty prelude to sex.

And he could honestly say that if enflaming was truly the goal, then he'd definitely succeeded in setting himself on fire.

Simply put, he wanted Sarah Jane.

He wanted to kiss her until she melted, taste the side of her neck, slide his tongue over her nipples and feast between her legs. Then he wanted to settle himself firmly in the womanly cradle of her thighs and plunge into her until they were both begging for release.

Unfortunately, dragging her into the convoluted mess of his life was simply out of the question. Kissing her had been bad enough, a breach of trust. Sleeping with her would leave his conscience in shreds. He had to resist her. For both their sakes, he really needed to do the right thing, although the right thing in his instance felt horribly, horribly wrong.

But there was one thing he could fix, Mick thought, and he had every intention of doing that. Thankfully, Payne had given him the leeway to make his own choices regarding this case, and unbeknownst to Chastity, Mick was switching sides.

He just wasn't going to tell the woman until after he'd found Sarah Jane's father's will.

When had he decided this was the right course of action? Who knew? But it was, all the same. If Chastity was willing to go to the expense of hiring them—with money that wasn't rightfully hers, Mick thought darkly—and hide her husband's will, then she was fully capable of following through with her threat to have Sarah Jane put back in jail.

Not on his watch, he decided.

He opened his cell once more and keyed in Huck's number.

"Finn," his friend answered by way of greeting.

Mick outlined the situation for him, alerting him to the change in facts as he knew them. "She's sleeping with the attorney who Sarah Jane says drafted the will," he said. "According to the local banker, she's withdrawn a sizable amount of cash for a deposit on a vacation home. She's breezing through the money like it's growing on a damned tree, as though she wants to spend as much of it as she can before the will surfaces. Frankly, I suspect we were hired to keep Sarah Jane from finding the will, *not* to keep her from stealing things from the house." He snorted. "As far as Chastity's concerned, that's just a little bonus."

Huck swore. "You've got full discretion on this, Mick. If you think it's time to pull the plug, then by all means let's do it. Ranger Security doesn't want any part of this. We'll quietly withdraw."

Mick winced, uncertain how to proceed. "If it's all the same to you, I'd like to keep Chastity in the dark for a little while longer and do some poking around."

Bad metaphor, he thought as a beat slid into three.

"So long as you know what you're doing," Huck said, a hint of warning in his voice.

He didn't, precisely, Mick thought as he snapped the phone shut.

A fateful smile slid over his lips. But when had that ever stopped him?

9

"PLEASE, PLEASE, PLEASE tell me that Mason has gotten in touch with you," Tina said, her voice a beleaguered combination of worry and dread.

Sarah Jane felt her heart jolt into overdrive. "What? Is he okay? He was sick today and went home, but I didn't think it was anything ser—"

"No, no, no." Tina hurriedly reassured her. "It's not that. He's fine. I mean, he's sick, but not any sicker than he was when you saw him earlier."

Confused, Sarah Jane frowned. "I'm afraid I'm not following. If he's okay, then why has he been trying to get in touch with me?"

Tina released a weary sigh. "Sarah Jane, where is your cell phone?"

She glanced down. "On my coffee table."

"Is there any particular reason you didn't take it with you?"

She felt a smile flirt with her lips. Tina knew she'd gone out with Mick, so that should be obvious. "Because I didn't want to be interrupted."

"When I tell you what I'm about to tell you, you're going to *wish* you'd been interrupted."

Uneasiness trickled down her neck. "Tell me what?"

"Are you sitting down?"

Oh, hell, she thought, stomach roiling. "Do I need to?"

"Yes. Also remove any sharp objects and promise me that you will not flip out. You have to come up with an appropriate response. No attacking anybody. Promise?"

"If it's bad enough that you think I might attack somebody, then you ought to know I can't make that kind of promise, Tina. Just tell me what it is. You're scaring me."

"There's no need to be scared. You're just going to be mad as hell."

Mad was definitely preferable to scared. She did "mad" quite well, in her opinion. In fact, she was bloody brilliant at it. She sank down onto her couch, but remained on the edge of the seat. "Okay. I'm ready. What's the news?"

"Tucker Mills overheard some interesting gossip today while he was cleaning Chastity's pool. When he stopped by Mason's this afternoon to drop off some chicken soup, he shared it with him."

Tucker was one of Mason's good friends and one of the most active gossips in town. He often passed along little tidbits via her assistant. It was how she'd learned that Chastity had gotten the tummy tuck. Sarah Jane felt her mouth go dry and a horrible feeling settled into her belly. "Go on."

"Seems that Chastity was on her cordless phone, roasting poolside, talking to one of her friends—Laura probably—about how her 'secret weapon' had arrived in town."

She frowned. "Secret weapon?"

"Yep. Her secret weapon is a hired dick who's supposed to catch you trying to break into her house to find your father's will. He's supposed to document the evidence so that she can turn it over to the sheriff's department and have you arrested." Through the phone, Sarah Jane heard her friend's teeth grind. "Again."

It was true, she decided as she shot up from the couch and began to pace. Blood *could* boil. "That scheming bitch. I'll kill her. I'll pull her hair from its bleached-blond roots. I'll—"

"Sarah Jane, sit back down." Tina hesitated then, implying that the worst hadn't come.

She drew up short and blinked. "How did you know I was standing up?"

"Because I know you," Tina said, exasperated. "Now sit!"

Impatient, Sarah Jane shoved her hair away from her face. "Tina, if I can't throw things or hit somebody, you're going to have to let me pace."

She heard Tina release another sigh, as though she truly dreaded what she had to say. "Her private dick is a photographer, Sarah Jane. Who's posing as an employee from a magazine."

It took precisely three seconds for the relevance of that last sentence to penetrate Sarah Jane's consciousness, and when it did, she wished she'd listened to her friend and sat back down. Because her legs suddenly felt as if they were going to buckle.

"Mick?" she breathed. Surely not. There had to be some sort of mistake.

"She didn't mention him by name, but after seeing

them together this morning… I don't know. But I can't think of anyone else it could be, can you?"

Sarah Jane walked over to a chair, nudged Blinken aside and sat down heavily, reeling from the news. Though she desperately wanted to believe otherwise, in her heart she knew her friend was right. She hadn't really questioned the *Designing Weekly* article. She'd just completed a nice job for an Atlanta-based company prior to that call, and figured word had gotten to an editor at the magazine. But Sarah Jane *had* thought the photographer arriving on scene before the writer was a bit strange. Then seeing Mick with Chastity this morning… Hadn't she caught a weird vibe then? Hadn't she known something wasn't right?

Instead of listening to her instincts, she'd chalked up the reaction to jealousy—which, gallingly, God help her, was partly true—and had set about claiming him for herself.

Her cheeks blazed right along with her temper and her humiliation reached critical levels when she re-membered flirting shamelessly this afternoon, then asking Mick out. Her face suddenly crumpled in horror.

And oh, God, she'd kissed him. She'd been practi-cally sucking his face off and sliding all over him. If it hadn't been for Chase, things could have gone past the point of no return… Her eyes narrowed into angry slits. *And he'd known. He'd known, the scum-sucking, sleazy, miserable bastard.*

No doubt Chastity did, as well, which made it all the more unbearable. Sarah Jane's eyes suddenly burned. In anger, she told herself. She would not shed a tear over their deception. She would not be the butt of their joke.

Too late, a little voice chided. *Too damned late.*

She would not mourn the loss of what she'd thought might be the beginning of something special. Just because she'd felt more alive and more relaxed with him than she ever had with anybody else was no reason to cry. Mick Chivers had been part of Chastity's evil plan, a knowing participant. So what if Sarah Jane had felt a spark? A glow of something truly special?

It wouldn't have mattered, anyway; she knew he would never stay here. Hadn't she prepared herself for that? Hadn't she known she needed to guard her heart?

"Say something, Sarah Jane," Tina said.

She jumped, having forgotten the phone was pressed to her ear, then sighed heavily. "I don't know what to say, other than I feel like a total fool."

"How were you to know she'd stoop to something so low?" Tina demanded. "Who could have predicted this? You're not psychic, Sarah Jane. And this… This has all gone too far. I knew she didn't want you to find the will, but going to these lengths to keep you away from it? Either she hates you more than we knew, or your dad put something in that will she doesn't want you to see."

"Probably a combination of both." It really didn't make sense. Yes, Chastity was a mean-spirited slut, but there was something more to this move. The eternal question, of course, was *what?*

"Forewarned is forearmed, though. You're going to have to be really careful when you break into the house, because we now know you're being watched. The asshole," Tina muttered. "He sure had me fooled. I actually liked him."

She had, too, Sarah Jane thought glumly, her lips still tingling from his kiss.

"Anyway, while Tucker was eavesdropping, he also heard her mention that she was going over to Atlanta for a 'procedure' tomorrow morning and wouldn't be back until next Thursday. Sounds like some substantial—and expensive—work, doesn't it?" Tina said bitingly.

That was just the break she'd been waiting for, Sarah Jane realized, chastising herself for not staying on task. Instead of thinking about Mick's beautiful lips and that hopeful but futile ember of something extraordinary between them, she should have been thinking about getting her inheritance back before it was all gone. The longer Chastity hid the will, the more time she had to deplete Sarah Jane's funds.

She flexed her jaw. She didn't give a damn if Mick was watching her or not—she'd still do what she had to do. And if she had to slug him in the process, then so be it.

"So…what are you going to do about him?" Tina asked.

"What do you mean?"

"Are you going to let him know you know who he is, or are you going to blast him into next year?"

For the first time, Sarah Jane felt the ghost of a smile on her lips. "You mean I have to choose one?"

Her friend chuckled. "That's my girl. Seriously, though, what are you going to do?"

"You know, Tina, as much as I would like to play it the smart way, going along with this little farce so that I can keep an eye on him, as well…I just don't think

I'm that good an actress." She gave a little groan. "Particularly after tonight."

Her friend winced. "Dammit, I was afraid of that. How far did it go?"

"Just a kiss," she said, downplaying the massive groping session that had rocked her world a few minutes ago. And it had been so much more than a kiss. It had been wonderful, fantastic, moving…unforgettable. She'd seen stars and rainbows behind her eyelids. It was hands down the best kiss she'd ever had. Even knowing what she knew now, God help her, she still longed for another.

"So you're going to send him packing, right?"

"I am."

"Sweetie, I'm sorry." Tina tutted under her breath consolingly. "I know you liked him."

Sarah Jane grimaced as another altogether unpleasant realization surfaced. "I also liked the idea of being featured in *Designing Weekly* and the cash I was going to pick up, but it turns out that's a figment of my imagination, as well."

"I thought about that," Tina admitted. "It was a terrible thing for them to do."

Sarah Jane paused, gathered her indignation around her and straightened, hoping to dislodge a bit of the hurt. It really *was* a terrible thing. Wasn't it bad enough that Chastity was running through her inheritance like a redneck with a sudden influx of cash? Now she'd decided to mess with her business, as well? Her very livelihood? And he'd gone along with it? To collect money, indirectly, through *her?*

Sarah Jane set her jaw so hard she thought she heard her teeth crack.

"Let me know when you figure out what sort of punishment you're planning for Mick, because I might want a p-piece of the a-action for Chase."

The tremble she heard in Tina's voice immediately forced Sarah Jane's brain to switch gears. "What are you talking about? What's happened?"

"Chase has started seeing Laura again."

"Oh, Tina," she said, an apology in her voice. *That bastard,* she thought. Mick might not be the only person she was going to slug. "You've got to be kidding."

She heard a sob over the phone. "I wish I was. Clara saw them at a movie in Ridgeville last night. You know, Sarah Jane, I just don't get it. If he doesn't want me, why does he string me along?"

Because he's a selfish bastard. "Because he's not certain he *doesn't* want you. He's just sure that he doesn't want anyone else to have you."

Tina sniffled. "I just wish I knew what to do."

"You know what I think," Sarah Jane gently reminded her. "You break off completely and throw a little competition into the mix. He'll either let you go— and you'll know once and for all how he feels—or he'll come running back. Right now, he's calling the shots, and that suits him just fine. You've got to take charge. You can't keep *permitting* him to do this to you."

"You know what, Sarah Jane? You're right." She heard Tina blow her nose into a tissue. "I've known you were right all along, I just haven't wanted to execute your advice because it feels like giving up, and giving up is going to break my heart. But guess what? It's already broken. He breaks it every time he pulls something like this. Every time he hooks up with that sleazy vindictive whore. I'm done," she announced with more conviction than Sarah Jane had ever heard before. "I am *so* not letting him do this to me again."

Sarah Jane inwardly gave a little cheer. *Finally.* "I promise you won't regret it," she declared.

Tina sniffed again. "I wonder if you'll be saying that when I'm bawling on your shoulder."

"You can bawl on my shoulder anytime and you know it," she said, smiling.

"Men are turds," Tina announced.

"You know why, don't you?"

"No, why?"

Sarah Jane grinned as a vengeful plan, so perfect it might have been delivered from a genuine Revenge Muse, struck her. "Because they're full of shit."

Tina managed a watery chuckle. "There is that."

"Are you busy right now?" Sarah Jane asked in a deceptively light tone. "Got anything planned for the rest of the evening?"

"No," her friend said hesitantly. "Why?"

"Because I have the perfect remedy for their constipation. You game?"

A wicked laugh bubbled over the line. "You bet."

10

"Good morning, Mick," Tina said in a voice that was entirely too chipper for this hour of the day. She stood outside his bedroom door, holding a pretty basket of…something.

"Good morning," he replied groggily, surprised at her visit. He looked back over his shoulder and squinted at the bedside clock, blearily bringing it into focus. It was 5:00 a.m. *Five.* What the hell?

"I hate to bother you this early—"

Could have fooled him, Mick thought. In fact, she didn't look as if she hated it at all. Her lips were curved into a curiously happy yet strangely…malevolent grin.

"—but I wanted to give you this before I start breakfast this morning. Sarah Jane and I did some baking last night and she wanted you to have these." Tina extended the basket. "Homemade brownies. And she wanted me to let you know that she's had an unexpected call about a Victorian mantel and won't be at the Milton Plantation until around noon. She didn't want you to get out there and have to wait on her," Tina confided, rocking back on her heels. "Mason's still sick."

The rich scent of chocolate filled his nostrils. She'd baked for him? Really? he thought, pleased beyond reason as a sleepy smile slid over his lips. Had any woman ever baked for him? His grandmother had, of course, but no one else that he could recall. Odd that the domestic act should mean so much to him, but he was ridiculously delighted. An image of Sarah Jane clothed in nothing but an apron, with a chocolate-covered spoon in her hand, rose in his mind, making a snake of heat coil in his loins.

"Thanks," Mick said, looking forward to sampling one.

"I'll let you go back to bed," Tina told him. "And just think, now you can sleep in." She winked at him.

An excellent idea, Mick thought drowsily. He nodded his thanks to Tina, scarfed down a brownie, then found his pillow once more. Considering he'd had another late night making sure she didn't do anything that would land her beautiful ass in jail, he could do with a few more winks. He'd actually seen Tina arrive at Sarah Jane's shortly after he'd supposedly left. He'd known they were in the kitchen cooking something up, but he imagined they'd been working on fried-pie recipes. Sarah Jane had mentioned that Tina was going to enter the competition this year, as well.

At any rate, he thought, tucking a blanket more firmly around him, he knew he wasn't ready to leave his bed just yet. And when he awoke several hours later, only the promise of another brownie, followed by another fabulous breakfast—honestly, he'd eaten better in the past two days than he'd done in his entire life—

and then seeing Sarah Jane, propelled him from beneath the covers.

Staunchly ignoring the sensation that he was once again being watched, Mick muttered, "Keep your hands to yourself," to the resident ghost, then quickly showered, dressed and made his way downstairs. The dining room was empty, and when he poked his head into the kitchen to inquire about breakfast, he found Tina handing a basket to Chase, the policeman from last night. It was identical to the one Sarah Jane had given him.

"Sorry to interrupt," Mick said. He directed a hopeful smile at Tina. "I'm afraid I slept through breakfast. Would there happen to be anything left?"

Tina cocked her dark head with a regretful expression. "No, sorry."

Chase shot her a strange look. "But I just saw—"

She stomped on his foot, eliciting a surprised grunt from him. "That's for Clara."

Seemingly baffled, Chase winced and darted her an irritated frown. "Oh. Sorry."

"Have a brownie," Tina suggested. "They're excellent. I just gave a basket to Chase."

The cop smiled down at her intimately. "You keep cooking for me like this and I'm going to get fat."

"They're low calorie. All the goodness, none of the guilt."

He grinned at her. "In that case, I'll eat them all."

"That was the point," Tina said.

Feeling a bit like an intruder, Mick bade them goodbye, made the return trek upstairs for his brownies—he could do a lot worse for breakfast, he decided—then, after stopping for a bottle of milk to wash down all the chocolate, made his way out to the Milton Plantation. Granted, Sarah Jane wouldn't be there for a couple of hours, but he knew what needed to be done. He could get a bit of a head start in helping her out, particularly since Mason was still under the weather.

A little envelope on the screen of his cell phone indicated he had a voice mail—he must have missed the call while he was showering—so he quickly dialed in and listened to the message.

"Hey, man. It's Huck. Just got a call from Chastity that she's going to be out of town through next Thursday. I thought that might buy you the time I suspect you were looking for." He chuckled softly. "Also, the *Designing Weekly* piece is a go and they've agreed to use your photos. Thought you'd want to know that. They're going to get in touch with Sarah Jane in the next couple of weeks, so that the spread will run in the issue we'd told her. I know you're officially off the case, but keep me in the loop, will you?"

Pleased, Mick snapped the phone shut. Excellent, he thought. On more than one level. Sarah Jane wouldn't lose the business she'd counted on and, with Chastity out of town, he'd have an opportunity to search her house. Things were falling into place nicely, he decided, feeling better about the situation as a whole.

He pulled up to the front of the house and powered down his windows so the interior wouldn't turn into an oven—moot point in hundred-plus-degree heat, he supposed—then grabbed what was left of his brownies and milk and made his way inside.

He picked up a hammer and set to work removing

the oak paneling in the dining room, where they'd left off yesterday. It took precision, extreme care and strength, and the idea that he was saving something from certain ruin—something handmade and beautiful that had stood the test of time for more than a hundred years—made his chest swell with a quiet sense of pride.

He wiped a bead of sweat from his brow, ignoring a sudden stomach pain. No doubt he should have foregone a few of the brownies, but in absence of breakfast he'd pretty much decimated the entire basket. He carefully pried a section of panel loose from the wall, growing more confident and more relaxed with each successful piece. Now this was work, Mick decided, the thrill of purpose chugging through his veins.

This he could get used to.

THIS WOULD HAVE BEEN *so much easier if he'd had a shirt on,* Sarah Jane thought as she silently watched Mick stack the last piece of paneling onto the pile in the corner. Sweat glistened off of muscles she'd touched last night, but hadn't seen, and the sight…oh, the sight of them literally made her mouth water.

And there it was, she thought, spying the tattoo he'd told her he didn't know her well enough to show her…yet. Lord, how she'd looked forward to that. Only she'd imagined it would have come via an act a little more intimate than just watching him work with his shirt off. But there it was, on his shoulder—an eagle. Given the solitary aura that surrounded him, it seemed completely fitting. And damn her traitorous body, sexy as hell.

But then, so was the rest of him.

He was tall and broad, but lean and splendidly proportioned. *A mustang,* she thought again, wishing that,
a) she didn't still want him and b) he hadn't turned out
to be a scheming, lying, in-cahoots-with-Chastity
bastard. Sarah Jane's chest ached with the weight of the
betrayal. However short-lived, it still hurt because, just
like Ponder Hill, she'd begun to spin dreams about him.
And her irritation returned full force when she realized
she was literally subsidizing her own downfall. Her
eyes narrowed.

Thanks to him.

She felt a perverse jolt of glee as she watched him
wince in pain and rub his belly. Then she allowed him
to work a few more minutes—after all, she was paying
him, wasn't she?—before revealing her presence.

He'd made remarkable progress in the dining room,
having almost finished it, and though it galled her to
admit it, she found herself reluctantly impressed. Rather
than just rushing in and stripping the room, he'd taken
time and almost reverent care with the work, inspecting each board and section for damage or weak spots
before beginning the salvage.

Frankly, Mason didn't have the strength or the
finesse to do the job, and though she'd let a few younger
carpenters help her in the beginning, they'd always been
too eager and had done more damage than good.

Since then, she'd forgone working with a partner
because she knew she was an exacting boss. But
strangely, in an ironic, evil twist of fate, she'd thought
she could actually work with Mick. She'd even enjoyed
herself yesterday when he'd returned from taking
Mason home, and had helped her. It had been nice and,

much to her regret, had inspired a series of if-only thoughts, first and foremost being if only he'd stay.

But it had all been a lie, given his purpose here.

Speaking of which, it was time to put a stop to that. Sarah Jane stepped into the room and resisted the urge to return his smile. It looked so genuine, so open, intimate, and his mouth… She swallowed back a whimper. She loved his mouth. Loved that little crooked upper lip and the way it made his cheek crease with an endearingly sexy dimple. But she wouldn't be deceived again.

She couldn't afford to be. Literally.

Clearly, he was just a really good actor who'd gotten into his part.

And into her mouth and almost into her bed, which would have undoubtedly let him into her heart. Thankfully, Chastity hadn't been able to keep her gloating piehole shut, thereby preventing the worst. Yes, Sarah Jane's pride was wounded, but at this point, she was less disappointed and more angry. And anger was good. It had the bullying ability to push every other emotion aside until she had the time to deal with it.

"Hey," he said, his gaze falling to her mouth, causing her traitorous lips to tingle. "Thanks for the brownies."

"You enjoyed them?" She kept her tone deceptively light.

"I ate every one."

Sarah Jane winced in regret and strolled over to inspect his work. "You're going to wish you hadn't done that."

He twirled the hammer, still grinning. "Aw, Tina said they were low calorie, so I'm not worried about it."

She crossed her arms over her chest and made a false moue of concern. "That's not what I'm talking about."

His smile still in place, he switched the hammer to the other hand. "Oh?"

Sarah Jane looked up and met his gaze directly. She had the pleasure of watching a flicker of trepidation form there. "I know who you are and why you're here, Mick."

There was a momentary flash of guilt in his eyes before they grew guarded. An uneasy laugh bubbled up his throat. "I'm afraid I don't follow."

She chewed the inside of her cheek, struggling to stay calm. "You don't? Well, then, let me illuminate the facts to you as I know them. You're not from *Designing Weekly*—thanks for that, by the way," she added. "It's nice to know I've done all this prep work for nothing, and the money I was expecting isn't going to come."

"I—"

"You are working as a private investigator for Chastity, and you've been charged with the task of catching me breaking into *my own house* to find my father's will so that I can claim my inheritance before my thieving slut of a stepmother runs through every bit of it and sells off my home to subsidize her future plastic surgery. If I understand things correctly, the only reason you've brought a camera along is to document the evidence of my so-called crime."

Sarah Jane paused, staring at him. "Have I left anything out, Mick?" She rolled her eyes and snorted as if this was all laughable, as if she wasn't hurt and angry, as if she hadn't felt a spark of something special between them, something more substantial than sexual attraction. "If Mick is even actually your real name."

He didn't try to deny a single part of her story,

silently confirming his guilt. He merely looked away, rubbed the back of his neck and swore.

"Now, I realize that I'm actually paying for your services—by proxy, of course," she added sweetly. "But if it's all the same to you, I'd just as soon you earn your keep somewhere else. I've got work to do."

"Sarah Jane, listen—"

She stepped forward and very deliberately took the hammer out of his hand. "I've finally figured out your Indian name, Mick. Wanna hear it?"

He grimaced comically, making the moment particularly sweet. "Somehow I doubt it."

"It's Squatting Snake in the Grass."

His brows drew together in a questioning line. "*Squatting* Snake?"

She pretended to be thoughtful. "Last night it was just Snake in the Grass, but today…" She felt her lips twitch. "I think adding the 'squatting' is going to be particularly *significant*."

His belly gurgled ominously and his suspicious gaze narrowed. "What—"

"I'm so glad you liked those brownies. You're right. They're not the kind that'll truly stick to your ribs because I added a secret ingredient just for you." She smiled evilly. "Those mocha chunks in there? Did you notice them?" She didn't wait for him to answer. "Those were actually chocolate laxatives."

Gratifyingly, his eyes widened in horror. "No," he said, laughing nervously even as his stomach made another interesting sound. "You didn't." He swallowed, the muscles in his throat moving uneasily.

"Why wouldn't I?" she asked. "Because it was

underhanded and vindictive?" She frowned pointedly. "Like you."

"Sarah Jane—"

"I'd hurry if I were you," she said, cutting him off once again. "I'm sure you've noticed there's no bathroom out here, and if you ate all of them like you've claimed to…" She shrugged, leaving the rest unsaid, and winced regretfully. "It's a long drive back to town."

Looking a bit pale and more sweaty than he had a few minutes ago, Mick grabbed his shirt and shrugged into it. He pulled his keys from his front jeans pocket and sent her a comically pained but determined look. "This conversation isn't over."

"The hell it's not," she retorted. "Stay away from me, Squatting Snake in the Grass. We're done." She summoned a sweet, patently false grin just for his benefit. "Enjoy your afternoon. I believe Clara keeps a stack of magazines in the common room."

"I'll see you later," he promised, completely ignoring her. He was a man, after all, she thought, watching him awkwardly slide into his SUV and roar out of the driveway as though he was being chased by the hounds of hell. She smiled. Or, more accurately, the *bowels* of hell.

Either way, she meant what she'd said. They were done.

Fool me once, shame on you. Fool me twice, shame on me. And as Mason had said yesterday, Sarah Jane was nobody's fool.

Not even a good-looking, lonely mustang's, who made her heart long for things it had never wanted and her body burn like dry tinder touched by a lit match.

11

MICK SPENT the better part of the afternoon and early evening doing exactly what Sarah Jane had intended for him to do—the evil, spiteful she-devil—so by the time he got back out to the Milton Plantation to speak to her again, she'd left for the day. *Squatting Snake in the Grass,* he thought ruefully, his poor stomach still a bit queasy.

Of all the fiendish, diabolical things. Laxatives in the brownies. He snorted. He'd heard of the prank before, of course, but had never carried out or been on the receiving end of such a heinous personal attack…until now.

Tina, the she-devil's partner in crime, had evidently been on the lookout for him, because when he'd rushed into the B and B, she'd been leaning against the doorjamb, all sweet and smug. If Chase's brownies had been infected, as well, then Mick certainly felt for the man. He could empathize.

Literally.

Still, for all his moaning and groaning and bellyaching—and he meant that in the truest sense of the word—there was a small part of him that was reluctantly impressed with her prank. He couldn't help it. It was a hell-raiser thing, a mutual respect for a trick well played…and Sarah Jane Walker had executed it brilliantly.

Catching him off guard early in the morning, devising a plan to be late getting to work, thereby allowing him to sleep through breakfast. And he'd followed her carefully laid trail one crumb at a time, devouring her payback brownies every step of the way.

A quick check at her house now revealed her truck in the driveway, but after ten minutes of knocking on her door, Mick got the impression that she truly wasn't home. Of course, she could simply be avoiding him, but for whatever reason, he didn't think that was the case. Sarah Jane liked a good row. Hiding from him when he knew she'd secretly like to throttle him didn't seem her style.

Call him crazy—and many people certainly had—but he was actually glad that she'd found him out. Being deceitful had never been his style. Had he intended to tell her about his original purpose? Truthfully, no. He'd planned to keep her out of trouble until he could find the will, and use the magazine article cover to keep working with her. Why? Because he selfishly wanted to spend more time with her, even knowing that it wasn't prudent. Even knowing that being with her without *being* with her was tantamount to torture.

As much as he hated to admit it, Mick feared he'd developed a bit of an…attachment to her.

Considering that she didn't particularly like him at

the moment, that wasn't smart. In this messed up stage of his life, developing an attachment to anything probably wasn't wise. Especially when, he suddenly realized, his heart had become involved.

No, he had to be mistaken, Mick decided. This was a sizable amount of admiration coupled with a monumental quotient of lust. She was novel. Unique. And he was in a compromised condition, that whole ship-without-a-rudder thing. He'd completely lost perspective, that was all.

Rather than sit outside her house, waiting on her to make the next move, Mick decided to take advantage of Chastity's absence and go over to Sarah Jane's old home. He pocketed a penknife and a flashlight, then parked a couple of blocks away and quickly made his way around back. The gate was locked, but was easily picked. *At last,* he thought. Ranger training was coming in handy.

The back door on the old Victorian was new, but the lock was even easier to disengage. Using the flashlight, Mick decided to make a quick sweep of the house to learn the layout, as well as to make sure he was alone before beginning an in-depth search. The first floor revealed a kitchen, utility room, parlor—where, in a crime against home decor, Chastity had installed a tanning bed—formal living room, dining room and half bath.

The second floor contained three bedrooms, two full baths and what Mick instinctively knew had to be Sarah Jane's father's study. The room smelled of cherry-tobacco smoke and housed a big desk and leather chair. Books lined the walls, filling the built-in shelves. He'd spotted a filing cabinet and decided that would be the best place to begin his search when a noise from the adjacent bedroom—Sarah Jane's old room, he imagined, given the purple frilly bedspread—caught his attention.

Instantly alert, he switched off the flashlight, doubled back and covertly made his way to her old room. Adrenaline kicked his heart rate into overdrive and made the skin on the back of his neck prickle as he heard the noise again—coming from the window, he was sure. He crept closer, then peeked around the edge and waited, certain he'd caught a glimpse of something outside. A break in the clouds released a shaft of moonlight and that's when he saw her.

Or her hair, rather.

Chuckling softly, Mick shone his flashlight through the glass, illuminating Sarah Jane's irritated face. Firm chin, narrowed eyes. Totally mutinous. Only he would find that intensely sexy. She clung to a tree branch a few feet from the window and glared poison-tipped daggers at him.

Mick opened the window and leaned nonchalantly against the sill, as though seeing her in a tree was an everyday occurrence. "Fancy meeting you here," he whispered.

"What the hell are you *doing?*" Sarah Jane asked, her voice low and harsh. Dressed all in black, she wiggled farther out on the limb, causing the branch to make a threatening crack. That accounted for the noise.

Mick frowned. "You'd better go back. That limb's not going to hold."

"Yes it will," she snapped. "I know what I'm doing.

I've climbed this tree dozens of times." Predictably ignoring his advice, she carefully inched closer, and the branch gave another groan in protest.

"As an adult?" Mick asked, growing more concerned by the second. "Seriously, Sarah Jane. Climb down and I'll let you in the back door."

A bark of ironic laughter broke from her throat. "So that you can take a picture of me for Chastity? I don't think so."

Mick exhaled an impatient sigh and helpfully pointed out the flaw in her logic. "If I was going to take a picture of you, I'd have already done it. I don't even have my camera." He glared at her. "Now get the hell out of that tree before you fall and crack your beautiful skull and I'll *let you in the back door.*" The last bit came out more as a growl than actual words.

Sarah Jane paused, seemingly unaccustomed to being told what to do, and Mick belatedly realized his demand was tantamount to waving a red flag in front of a bull. She simultaneously lifted her chin and a single haughty eyebrow, and said, "I'm coming through the window."

It had been so long since someone had disobeyed his direct order, Mick was momentarily stunned.

She heaved an exasperated breath. "So, if you're not going to help me, then at least get the hell out of the way," she snarled, taking hold of the screen to pull it loose.

Leaping into action, Mick swore and popped the screen out. Sarah Jane caught it and helped him angle it through the window, and he propped it against the wall. When he looked back, she was already halfway through the opening.

Determined to help her—because it seemed vitally important at the moment—he grabbed hold of her beneath her arms and tugged, sending both of them tumbling to the floor where they landed with a grunt. Her knee came perilously close to Dick and the Twins, but it was the feel of her lush body, those delectable breasts pressing against his chest, that made him unable to breathe.

Soft womanly body, apple-scented hair against his cheek, his hellcat, his she-devil…

He bit back a blistering curse as his body instantly reacted. His dick sprang to attention and nudged, recognizing that the proper anatomy was in line, even if it was still fully clothed.

Sarah Jane angled up, bracing her hands on either side of his head, and her startled gaze tangled with his. Her own breathing was quick and shallow, as though she, too, was aware of every part of her body currently pressed against his. She blinked, then inhaled sharply. Her eyes snapped with sudden insight and anger. "You were waiting for me, weren't you? Guarding the house to catch me?" With a disgusted breath and several garbled epithets, she rolled off of him and scrambled to her feet. "You low-down—"

"Squatting Snake in the Grass," he finished for her, standing, as well. "I believe we've covered that." His voice hardened. "Particularly the squatting part, thanks to you." And someone—either dear old Byron or Tina, he couldn't be sure—had sneaked into his room and removed all the toilet paper. He'd had to bellow from his bathroom like a toddler and ask for a replacement roll. Thankfully, Clara had discreetly taken care of it for him.

"I was going to say *bastard*," she said. "But you're right. Yours works better."

"Sarah Jane, I told you I didn't have my camera and I wasn't here guarding the damn house." He drew in a deep breath, hoping to inhale a little patience, as well. "If you could stop leaping to conclusions for just a minute, I'd like to explain."

She paused and he watched her cock her head in the darkness. "Oh, you mean you can explain working for Chastity? You can explain why, in order to line your pockets with my stolen money, you agreed to trap me so that the bitch ends up with everything that's supposed to belong to me? You can? Really?" she asked sarcastically. "Well, by all means, go ahead. I won't stop you. I'd really like to hear how you can *explain* that."

That wasn't exactly what he'd intended to explain. Come to think of it, *explain* probably wasn't the right term. *Defend his position* would probably work better. Mick scowled at her. "Has anyone ever told you that you're a smart-ass, Sarah Jane?"

"Yes, as a matter of fact, they have—"

He grunted, unsurprised.

"—but you've got the jackass title locked down tight, so no worries on that score." She flipped on her own flashlight, momentarily blinding him. "If you're not here to trap me, then what *are* you doing here?"

Mick squeezed his eyes shut, grabbed the end of her light and angled it out of his eyes. "I came here to look for the freakin' will. I'm trying to help you, dammit." He hadn't planned to tell her that, but she had a way of surprising things out of him.

Sarah Jane aimed her light to the right of his face, once again illuminating his expression. "*You* want to help *me?*"

Skepticism dripped from every word, showcasing just how hard he was going to have to work to convince her. He'd ventured behind enemy lines, survived countless high-risk missions and had managed covert operations he imagined were less difficult than winning over her trust.

But for whatever reason—insanity, he decided, smothering the pressing urge to howl—he felt he had more riding on this assignment than any other in his life.

Clearly, he'd lost his mind…and quite possibly a little piece of a vital organ farther south and to the left.

SARAH JANE WATCHED Mick's expression, looking for any hint of deceit. His unfairly handsome face, the one she'd committed to memory over the past few days, remained open and without the slightest evidence of dishonesty. Gut instinct told her he was earnest, but she didn't know how much to trust it. That could be wishful thinking brought about by intense sexual attraction and something else. Something less definable, but frightening all the same, that thing that had inspired all those if-onlys.

If only you wouldn't be bored out of your skull here…

If only you'd like to work with me…

If only you wouldn't leave and we could explore this thing happening between us…

If only you weren't damaged…

If only I could trust you not to break my heart…

That shadow of loneliness, of untold sorrow she'd periodically glimpsed in those unusual blue eyes, surfaced again, fraying her heartstrings and instilling the annoying but persistent urge to help him.

Her enemy…who claimed he wanted to help her. Talk about a quagmire.

Sarah Jane expelled a small, tired sigh. "Who are you, really? No bullshit, no lies. Bare-bones facts, please."

He considered her for a moment before answering. "I'm Mick Chivers. I'm former military, now working for Ranger Security based out of Atlanta, though after this assignment—my first, by the way," he added, chuckling darkly, "I'm resigning from their employ. I'm twenty-nine, originally from Kentucky, practice amateur photography, but don't work for *Designing Weekly*. Although they will do the spread on you as planned, and have agreed to use my photos, which is why I'll have to continue to take pictures while you finish the salvage project at the Milton Plantation. I'm allergic to shellfish, much to my regret, enjoy action-adventure movies, Southern rock and reading true-crime novels. I'm a registered Independent, nonsmoker, occasional drinker…and I like you, Sarah Jane." He paused just long enough for her to remember their kiss, making her intensely aware of the fact he was less than a foot away, shrouded in darkness. "Does that answer all of your questions?"

Not by a long shot, she thought, a reluctant smile pulling at her lips. "It's a start. So…this Ranger Security? Is this the first job you've had since you left the military? What branch were you in?"

"It is." There was a guarded tone in his voice, barely detectable, but there all the same. "I was in the army, a Ranger, specifically." She heard him swallow. "I served ten years."

Ten years and he'd walked away? she thought, struck

by the admission. From being a Ranger? Didn't it take years of special training to become one of the army's elite? Weren't those men usually in for life? Why would he do that? Sarah Jane wondered, intrigued. What would make him want to leave after all that time, all that training? She longed to ask, but instinctively knew better. Nevertheless, intuition told her that his recent misery had something to do with leaving the military. She knew it. Could feel it. "Why are you leaving Ranger Security?"

That chuckle came again, the one that slipped into her blood and inevitably made her smile. "Because I'm obviously not cut out for it. Just look at how I've botched this job. You were officially my target, Sarah Jane, and so far I've managed to abandon my mission in favor of taking up your cause—with Ranger Security's permission, of course—and become intimately involved with you. I'd say I've broken a couple cardinal rules, wouldn't you?"

"I wouldn't c-call it intimate," she stammered, feeling herself blush at his terminology. She inwardly squirmed. "It was just a kiss."

As though drawn by an invisible cord, he sidled forward, lessening the distance between them. "Just a kiss?" he said, his low voice laced with an undercurrent of…desperation? "I, uh, I think you need a little remedial instruction on what defines a kiss, sweetheart." He pressed his lips to the corner of her mouth, the gentle action making her eyelids flutter shut. "That's a kiss. Sweet, simple, a mere brush of my lips against yours." Every word he said made her melt and sway toward him. She was putty in his hands, utterly pathetic. She swallowed a whimper, and wished she could resist him.

For the first time in her life, she realized what her friend Tina must feel like around Chase. To be a hopeless slave to her body, her heart.

Mick framed her face with his warm palms, drawing her close. "This… This is a bit more intimate." He lingered over the last word, then fastened his lips to hers as though he'd been dying to taste her, that every breath away from her mouth was one wasted. This kiss was hungry, almost punishing, as though all of this—this attraction, these circumstances—were somehow her fault.

Oh, hell no, Sarah Jane thought, answering his unspoken challenge as her control literally snapped.

She wasn't taking the wrap for this. She kissed him back, her tongue dueling his. She dropped her flashlight, abandoning any pretense of restraint, and wrapped her arms around his neck, her legs around his waist. Propelled by her unexpected assault, he stumbled back against her old bed, taking her slowly down with him. He fed at her mouth, suckling her tongue, dragging her further and further down the slippery slope of desire.

In a small, dim corner of her mind, Sarah Jane suspected this was not the right path—sleeping with Mick was the height of idiocy. He was still possibly her enemy—though she sincerely doubted it. But he was definitely temporary, and more disturbingly, had the potential to break her heart.

Was it in danger at the moment? Probably not.

But a week from now when he was gone, when he left town never to return…who knew about then? Right now she skated the thin edge of being emotionally invested, but feared a single misstep or a single endearing crook of these devilishly talented lips could send her reeling into misery.

If she had a brain in her head, she'd retreat from this battle he'd started, stop tugging the shirt from the waistband of his jeans—

Hot bare skin, supple muscle...

She groaned low in her throat, a purr of pleasure, and her roaming palms feasted on his flesh.

She'd make him remove his wonderful hands from her ass, and she'd run as fast as she could back to her own house and barricade the door.

Unfortunately, her brain had already ceded control to the fever in her blood, the fight being enacted through sexual warfare, an ultimate winner-take-all war for the upper hand, and she knew she had a better chance of damming the Mississippi with Silly Putty than resisting him now.

Because she didn't want to.

She'd wanted Mick Chivers the instant she'd seen him. Had longed to feel him touching her like this, kissing her, heaven help her, *taking* her the way he was right now. He was laying siege and, while she was putting up a valiant fight, she would gladly lose if it meant she'd get to come apart in his arms. In fact, she'd gladly let him conquer the hell out of her. What was that old saying? Never take a hill you weren't willing to die on?

That's what this felt like. Laying it bare, giving it everything, lost and beyond caring... She couldn't help herself. She *couldn't* stop. She wanted him too desperately, temporary or not.

He dragged her shirt up and over her head, tossed it

aside, then quickly popped the front clasp of her bra. A second later, wonderfully sexy lips were on her pouting nipple, tugging it into the hot cavern of his mouth. Sarah Jane gasped, pleasure bolting through her, and set about removing his clothes, as well. Every cell in her being screamed for instant release, desperate to put the hardest part of him into the softest part of her. She could feel her pulse beating a steady tattoo in the heart of her sex, her folds slickening, readying for him.

More importantly, she could feel him beneath her, hot, hard and huge, nudging determinedly against her. She ripped the shirt from his body and flung it aside, then aligned herself more firmly against him, flexing her hips on the hard, jean-covered ridge of his arousal.

She whimpered, quivered as sensation whipped through her. It wasn't nearly enough. She needed to be closer.

As though reading her mind, Mick slipped his hands beneath her black leggings and panties and, not even bothering to unbutton or unzip, slid them over her rump. She wriggled, once, twice, helping him along, then kicked them off and onto the floor.

She was naked. He wasn't. But that was easily rectified, she thought, her hand going to the snap of his jeans. He drew in a startled breath, sucking his belly away from his waistband where the tip of his swollen penis sprang free. Her fingers brushed him as the zipper whined.

"Sonofabitch," he whispered.

She moved his boxers over his hips and out of the way, then took him in her hand and worked the slippery skin against her palm, milking a single bead of hot moisture from the tip. Emboldened, she swirled her finger over the top and heard him swear again, this time even more vehemently. Sarah Jane smiled. He'd wanted a war, hadn't he?

Before she'd even completed the thought, he had her on her back and was licking a determined path down her belly, his hands skimming over her sides, as though memorizing every indentation, every inch of skin. He paused at her belly button, slipping his tongue inside, even as his fingers brushed her soaked curls. It was as though his tongue had depressed a catch in her hips, making her legs fall open for him, baring herself to him.

Mick dragged a finger through her folds, unerringly honing in on the sensitive nub nestled at the top of her sex. He pressed a finger deep inside, then hooked his thumb around and knuckled her until her back bowed off the bed.

"Mick."

"Yes, Sarah Jane?" His voice was ladened with male confidence, and she imagined that sexy grin in the darkness.

"That's a n-neat trick. C-can you do it w-with something other than your f-finger?"

A wicked chuckle sounded, and a heartbeat later he was laving and suckling, lapping at the heart of her with his tongue.

Sarah Jane felt her eyes widen, her belly quake and a startled part gasp, part laugh tear from her throat. That wasn't what she'd meant, but sweet God, it would do. A shuddering breath leaked out of her lungs as the first flash of climax caught fire.

Seemingly sensing that she was close, Mick drew

back, hastily grabbed his jeans and withdrew a condom from his wallet. He tore open the packet with his teeth, fished the protection out and swiftly rolled it into place.

"Sarah Jane?"

Back to being chivalrous, was he? she thought, suppressing the wild urge to laugh. He'd just stripped her naked and tasted every intimate part of her. Did he have to ask?

She angled her hips up, brushing purposely against him. "Yes, Mick?"

He bent forward and sipped at her nipples, abrading her skin with his five o'clock shadow. "Can I come into you?" he asked, his voice low and hoarse with need.

She angled up against him once more, then bent forward and nipped at his shoulder, licked that delicate skin at the hollow of his throat. If she'd had a white flag, she would have waved it.

I surrender.

But her answer would have to suffice. "Yes," she breathed. "Come into me…and make me come," she added wickedly.

12

It was an absolute miracle that he didn't have a screaming orgasm right then, Mick thought, chuckling softly at her sinful command.

"You bet," he said. An instant later, he was inside of her, buried to the hilt in her welcoming folds. He groaned as her feminine muscles clamped around him, holding him in place. And even as his body demanded the exquisite friction of movement, everything inside him went still as a peace more fulfilling than anything he'd ever experienced swept through him, mending fissures, cleaning out the clutter stuck to his soul.

He felt strangely energized, but calm…*soothed,* Mick realized with a flash of insight, the thought so unique and profound he felt a curious tingling in the back of his throat.

For the first time in his life, he realized he was exactly where he was supposed to be.

With her. In her.

Sarah Jane wrapped her legs around his waist and

rocked beneath him, her greedy body absorbing his thrusts. He pushed deep and hard, then harder and faster and faster still. Her dark blond hair fanned out beneath her head, the moonlight picking up streams of caramel. Her soft breath whispered against his skin, her eager hands slid over his back and grabbed his ass, urging him on, as if she was desperate for the release that hovered just out of reach.

Funny, Mick thought. He'd wanted to punish her for belittling their kiss, when they'd both known it had been so much more. Kissing her had rattled him to the very core. How dare she say that it was "just a kiss"? That was like saying the Taj Mahal was just a building or the Atlantic was just an ocean. That kiss had shaken him to the soles of his feet, had made him abandon what was left of his good sense and his restraint and had made *her* priorities *his*.

But, too late, he saw the flaw in his reasoning—an occurrence that was happening with entirely too much frequency for his comfort. If merely kissing her had rattled what was left of his already imploding world, what the hell had he expected to happen when he made love to her? How could he have thought for an instant that it would just be sex? Just an attraction? How could he think that he'd walk away from her an unchanged man?

Because, Mick realized, as her heels dug into his ass, her beautiful breasts slid against his chest and her small hands lovingly mapped his back, desperate and reverent, eager and in awe, there was no way he'd ever be the same.

The knowledge should have spooked him, should have scared the hell out of him, because he'd never felt this way before. He'd never met a woman who simply did it for him the way Sarah Jane did. But Mick Chivers had never been afraid of anything in his life and he'd be damned if he'd start now. She was just a girl, he told himself as he pumped in and out of her, desperate to believe it.

She was just a girl…and he was just a guy who could quite possibly fall in love with her.

If he hadn't already.

Sarah Jane made a keening cry low in her throat and her neck arched back, even as her hips upped the tempo between them.

"Oh, Mick. I need—I want—"

Me, he mentally supplied. *You need me. You want me.*

She thrashed wildly beneath him, making little mewling sounds that, impossibly, made his swollen dick stiffen even more, just shy of the point of pain. His balls hardened until he thought they'd shatter. He could barely breathe, his lungs were so tight. He could feel his release gathering force in his loins, building and building, but refused to let it go until she'd gotten hers.

Make me come, she'd said. And he would, if it freakin' killed him.

With his heart threatening to pound right out of his chest, Mick reached down between their joined bodies and knuckled her clit once again. That teeny amount of pressure was all it took to send her flying over the edge.

Her back bowed off the bed, her mouth opened in a soundless scream and he could feel her tight little body closing around him, again and again, hard contractions that ultimately set him free, as well. The orgasm blasted from the back of his loins like a bullet down the barrel of a gun, and with each continuing pulse from her body, he quivered and shook. Gooseflesh raced up and down his spine, and it took every bit of strength he possessed not to completely collapse on top of her.

Hands down, it was the most incredible sex of his life.

And he knew why. He knew, though he didn't want to admit it, didn't want to even acknowledge what was happening to him.

The difference was her, Mick knew. Sarah Jane Walker, his hellcat, his she-devil. He chuckled softly, gently pressing a kiss to her cheek.

His little badass.

The question was…just what in the hell was he supposed to do with her? Particularly when he didn't know what he was going to do with himself.

"WELL, THIS IS CERTAINLY a significant change in events," Tina said, staring at Sarah Jane in wide-eyed astonishment. "You know, when you called this morning and said you were going to miss breakfast, I didn't think that much about it. I just thought you were staying home and licking your wounds." Her lips twitched. "But that wasn't the case at all, was it? You were too busy licking *him*."

Sarah Jane finished putting a coat of paint on the picket fence that would go around their Fried Pie Festival booth, and felt the tops of her ears burn. "Only after he came clean," she said.

Tina cocked her head in bemusement. "He came clean? Really? In my experience it's always been a little—" she gave a delicate shudder "—messy."

Struggling to keep a straight face, Sarah Jane glared at her friend. "Did you completely miss the part where

I said he was going to help me find the will? That he hadn't felt right about any of this since the beginning? That Chastity's evil plan has backfired because the lackey she thought she was hiring isn't a lackey at all, but a hero?" Sarah Jane quirked a brow, practically giddy at the thought. "Were you listening to me at all, or are you more interested in teasing me about the best sex I've ever had in my life?"

Tina dipped her brush once more. "Seriously? The best ever?"

"Tina."

"Fine." Her friend relented. "If you want to focus on the whole villain-to-hero aspect of this—which admittedly is pretty damned romantic—then I suppose that'll work for me." She slid her a look. "But it's still not as juicy as the sex news if you ask me."

Villain-to-hero aspect, Sarah Jane thought, secretly pleased with her friend's assessment. That certainly seemed fitting. Just a couple of days ago Mick had been the instrument of her destruction, but things had definitely changed.

And though they'd searched every nook and cranny of her old house—and she'd departed the premises with her mother's wedding dress, her father's pipe, as well as a few photo albums she'd wanted—and they still hadn't found the will, Sarah Jane felt confident that, together, they would.

As a matter of fact, next week during the festival, while Cecil was busily judging the competition, they planned to sneak away to search his office. With any luck they'd lay hands on it and be back at the town square by the time the winners were announced. In the meantime,

Chastity was going to be lulled into a false sense of security, imagining that her watchdog was in place, especially since Sarah Jane had every intention of spending most of her time next week with Mick. She grinned.

And so far, her plan was working out splendidly.

Though he hadn't stayed with her last night, Sarah Jane had every intention of asking him to do so tonight. She'd met him first thing this morning at the Milton Plantation and, despite several lengthy kisses, which led to some pretty intense sex, they'd managed to get an incredible amount of work done. No doubt she would finish ahead of time, which was better for everyone all around. Ervin's dozer schedule wouldn't be interrupted, and with Mick at her side for the next week, she'd encouraged Mason to take time off to scope out a few local colleges, something he'd been postponing in favor of working with her.

Though she'd always done the majority of the salvage work herself, Sarah Jane had to admit having a capable second on the job with her was…nice. Not to say that she didn't appreciate Mason—she did.

But Mick… Mick worked with the same care and efficiency that she did, and while she'd always loved her job, she had to admit she'd loved it more the past couple of days with him by her side. Why? A million little reasons—that crooked smile, the humor in those unusual blue eyes, the way his chocolate waves became more endearingly unruly as the day wore on. He was smart and funny and every once in a while—usually when he had the camera pointed at her—she'd catch him looking at her in a most peculiar way. One that made her heart swell with the bloom of something special.

Something rare.

How did she know this? Because she was giving him the same unsure can-I-trust-what-I'm-feeling? look.

When she'd said last night had been the best sex she'd ever had in her life, Sarah Jane hadn't been lying. Hands down, the absolute best sex ever. It had rocked her world, shook her universe, sent her sailing past cloud nine and back again.

But…it had been so much more than that.

Damn those if-onlys, she thought.

Mick Chivers, a damaged, restless, guarded island unto himself, a lonely mustang, former military, soon to be former security specialist, with seemingly no plans for the future, who'd spent more time at a boarding school than at home, who'd learned carpentry from his grandfather and never mentioned parents or siblings—a man she knew seemingly nothing about—had managed, with just a crook of those devastatingly sexy lips, to insinuate himself into her…affections.

No, as much as Sarah Jane would like to tell herself this was merely a harmless flirtation punctuated with magnificent sex, she knew better.

She knew herself better. For the first time in her life, she could look ahead and see a future—one that was as imaginary as the life she'd planned on Ponder Hill. Still, in her mind she could see him by her side in her dream house, them making love in the blue glow of stained glass beneath her wishing angel.

Unfortunately, she didn't know Mick as well as she knew herself. But with any luck that would soon change. Tonight, they planned to order a pizza, then

Sarah Jane had promised to show him the fine art of fried pie making. It was just an excuse, of course. She would have invited him over to watch paint dry if it meant she could spend another minute with him. Just knowing that he was leaving soon—an unspoken assumption—hung like a black cloud over their otherwise rosy new romance. But rather than think about that unpleasantness, she'd borrowed another page from Scarlett O'Hara's book and tried not to think about it. Tomorrow was another day. It wasn't the brightest or most mature tack, she'd admit, but she'd work with what she had.

And right now all she had was a limited time frame that was going to have to last her a lifetime.

"So no luck finding the will, then?" Tina asked, drawing her back into their conversation.

"None," she admitted, frowning darkly. "I think she's destroyed it." It was just the sort of thing Chastity would do. Her father's last wishes, tossed aside like so much garbage.

Tina's worried gaze met hers. "Surely to God Cecil has more sense than that."

"One would hope," Sarah Jane said with a shrug. "But you never know with men."

Her friend snorted. "You can say that again." She slid Sarah Jane a veiled look that instantly piqued her curiosity. "You're not the only one who had some interesting action last night."

"What?" Sarah Jane breathed. "Did you hear from Chase?"

Tina chuckled. "In a manner of speaking. He called and left a message on my machine, saying he'd be over after he 'finished spilling his intestines into our local sewer system' to have a little chat with me."

Sarah Jane choked on a laugh. She could just imagine his outrage. Served him right for hurting her friend.

"So I invited Mark Higgins over for dinner and served him my lemon artichoke chicken, roasted new potatoes, peas in white sauce and…" Tina's eyes twinkled with vengeful humor.

"Banana pudding," Sarah Jane finished breathlessly, awestruck at her friend's diabolical plan.

Chase's meal. His absolute favorite, the one Tina made only for him. If the way to a man's heart was indeed through his stomach, then watching another man enjoy his bounty had to have positively eaten Chase up.

"I'm so proud of you," Sarah Jane said, impressed. "That sounds like something I would do."

"I know." She squealed delightedly, apparently shocked at herself. "I opened every blind and every curtain in the dining room." She giggled. "Chase beat on the front door like an outraged elephant. It was wonderful."

"What did you do?"

"I calmly told him that I had a date and we were trying to enjoy our meal. If he was hungry or looking for company he could try 410 First Street."

Sarah Jane felt her eyes widen significantly. "Laura's address. Stroke of genius," she said, nodding. "Utterly brilliant."

Tina made a moue of regret. "I'm not sure how brilliant Mark thought it was. He knows how I feel about Chase." She gave a little miserable snort. "Hell, the whole town knows that."

"Don't worry about Mark," Sarah Jane told her. "He's always happy for a good meal. As for Chase...I'll bet he's questioning what he *knows* today."

Tina crossed her arms over her chest. "I hope you're right. He certainly seemed jealous."

"Has he called?"

"Several times. I've been ignoring him. He came by Clara's this morning and she wouldn't let him into the kitchen."

Sarah Jane grinned. "Excellent. I think this is just what he needs."

"I don't know about that, but it feels good to stop being the victim, I can tell you that." Tina smiled sadly. "I should have listened to you a long time ago."

Remembering the little insight she'd had last night about her friend's feelings, Sarah Jane shook her head. "Nah," she said. "I believe that everything happens in its own time for its own reason. Until now, you haven't been ready." She rocked back on her heels. "Now you are."

Tina's concerned gaze met hers. "What about you, Sarah Jane? Are you going to be 'ready' when Mick leaves town?"

Sarah Jane ignored the prick of uneasiness in her chest and shrugged. At this rate, Scarlett O'Hara wouldn't have enough pages in her book to matter. "Honestly, Tina, I'm trying not to think that far ahead."

"Whether you're thinking about it or not, it's coming." Tina winced, her face a mask of concern. "I just don't want to see you get hurt. I know that Mick's ended up being a really great guy—and I'm thrilled that he's going to help you—but that boy looks like the type who's always sitting on *G,* waiting on *O.*" She hesitated. "I guess what I'm trying to say is—"

Sarah Jane smiled sadly. "I know what you're trying to say, and I know, so no worries, okay? I know what I'm doing."

Lies, lies, all lies. She didn't have any idea in hell what she was doing. She just knew she couldn't stop.

13

MICK PLUCKED ANOTHER berry from the basket on Sarah Jane's kitchen counter and watched her carefully flip another fried pie. She wore a frilly apron over her trademark sleeveless shirt and shorts, her hair pulled into its usual ponytail. There was a smudge of flour on her adorable chin, and while he knew he should tell her about it or wipe it off himself, he thought she looked too damned cute.

One of her cats—Nod, if memory served—wound around her legs while she stood at the stove, and all three dogs lay sprawled under the kitchen table. Norah Jones's voice floated from an under-the-counter CD player, and the strong scent of cinnamon sugar flavored the air.

"All right," Sarah Jane said, transferring a warm pie onto a plate for him. "I'm a pie purist, which means I don't want any whipped topping or ice cream. However, if you'd like some, I have one or both."

Mick grinned. "A pie purist?"

Her answering smile was chiding. "Don't mock me. I told you we take our pie seriously around here."

He nodded and reached for the fork she handed him. "I remember."

She giggled, the sound vibrating through him. "You thought we were all crazy, didn't you?"

"I don't know where you would have gotten that idea."

Sarah Jane's lips curled. "You mean that 'I've-landed-in-Yokelville' look on your face wasn't supposed to tip us off?"

Mick carved off a chunk of flaky pie and lifted his chin. "I don't know what you're talking about. I've already told you that I was too busy staring at your ass to think about pie or anything else."

"You were facing me when we were talking about pie, boy genius."

He smiled evilly. "Sorry. I meant your breasts."

She gasped and whacked him with a dish towel. "Try it," she said, gesturing to his loaded fork.

Mick winked at her, then took a bite. Warm, sugary, the perfect blend between tart and sweet. *Like her,* he thought again. He groaned in pleasure and his gaze swung to hers. "This is wonderful," he said thickly. "No wonder you win every year."

"I haven't won every year," she said. "Just the past three." She smiled. "But I've got some new competition this year that I'm a little worried about."

"Oh, really? Who?"

She grinned. "Tina."

Mick inclined his head. "Ah. What sort of pie will Tina be entering?"

"I don't know. Though we've never kept secrets from each other in our lives, she's guarding her entry like it's the holy grail." Sarah Jane quirked her lips. "It's quite annoying of her, actually."

"Well, I don't care what she enters, you've got her beat."

"Thank you," she said, nodding primly. "I'm glad you like it."

"Seriously, Sarah Jane. It's fabulous." He took another bite. "Have you ever thought about trying to sell them through any of the local stores around here?"

She shook her head and a shadow passed behind her eyes. "Nah," she said. "This recipe belonged to my mother. It's a piece of my past, not a marketing strategy." She took a dishcloth and wiped down the counter. "This is just my way of honoring her, if that makes sense."

Mick swallowed. "Of course."

She turned to look at him. "What about you? Any family traditions?"

Before he could stop himself, he snorted. "Er...no." Mick glanced at her, then away. Damn, this was awkward. "I'm not what you'd call close to my parents," he admitted.

Her lips twisted. "I gathered that when you mentioned boarding school."

"I was...rambunctious," Mick said, glossing over the "bad seed" comment he'd once heard his father make. "And my parents weren't cut out to have kids. They're both college professors, scholarly, studious. They were always so wrapped up in their jobs and each other that I think I just—" he swallowed and gestured "—got in the way."

A flash of outrage lit her eyes, making something in his heart shift. "Bullshit. They became parents. They should have nurtured you, treasured you, not dubbed you a problem child and shipped you off to military school." She blushed, evidently fearing she'd overstepped her bounds. "Sorry," she said. "I know it's not my place—"

Mick waved his hand again, secretly pleased with her outrage on his behalf. He'd barely revealed the tip of the iceberg and she knew exactly what she was dealing with, right out of the gate. "It's fine. Water under the bridge."

"Maybe now, but I'll bet it nearly drowned you as a kid. Did you stir up a lot of trouble? Try to get sent home?"

He blinked, surprised. "Er…"

She lifted one slim shoulder in a shrug and smiled. "It's what I would have done."

"I did in the beginning," Mick found himself telling her, surprised at how easily the words were coming. "But then I'd get home and I'd be more miserable." His gaze found hers. "Believe it or not, it ended up being the best thing for me. I was always pulling some sort of prank, always getting in trouble. Hell, I told you what my nickname was, the one I got in Jump School."

"The Hell-raiser?" She nodded, and those gorgeous eyes, lit with humor, tangled with his. "I remember. And I can see where that would fit. You do seem a bit…restless."

"Restless?"

"Or as Tina says, 'sitting on *G*, waiting on *O*.'"

Mick laughed. "That's a new one."

"I have more."

"Why am I not surprised?"

"Hopefully, because I'm fascinating," she deadpanned, causing a bark of laughter to rumble from his chest.

"You are that, Sarah Jane," Mick said, sidling closer to her. He picked up a blackberry and fed it to her, felt his dick twitch as her ripe mouth closed around the succulent fruit. "And more."

Her gaze searched his. "Can I ask you something, Mick?"

He grimaced. "Usually that question is followed by a more personal one."

"It is personal," she admitted. "But I'm curious and it's not in my nature not to ask questions. You can reserve the right to refuse."

He nodded. "All right. Shoot."

"You said this was your first job since leaving the military. But you've never said *why* you left." She winced slightly, waiting for his response. "Too personal?"

Damn.

"No problem," she said, stepping away from him when he didn't respond. "Forget I asked. I just—"

"I screwed up," Mick admitted. "That's the short answer. Will that suffice?"

She studied his face and the flash of pity he saw in her eyes made him wonder what he'd revealed. He felt raw and open, as though she were delving into his thoughts, seeing things he wanted to keep hidden. "It will. Thank you."

"Tit for tat," Mick said. "I want to ask you something."

She shrugged. "Ask away."

"Last night…what made you decide to trust me?" He didn't know why her answer was important, but it was, and he'd been wondering about it all day. He'd deceived her six ways till Sunday and yet she'd still somehow managed to find merit in him. How?

Once again that penetrating gaze caught and held his. "Because you were so desperate for me to believe you, to believe *in* you. I knew you had to be telling the truth." She shrugged and offered a slightly wicked grin. "I was also hopelessly in lust with you, and sleeping with you seemed like an excellent consolation prize."

Another choked laugh got strangled in his throat. "C-consolation prize?" He'd been called many things in his life, but that was definitely a first.

"It seemed only fair," she said. "You'd put me through hell. I figured the least I should get was an orgasm out of it."

"Only one?" Mick said, playing along. "I was a total bastard. I think I owe you more than one, don't you?"

Sarah Jane picked up the basket of blackberries and a can of whipped cream and started out of the kitchen. She shot him a sidelong glance and grinned. "You don't really think you're here just to eat pie, do you?"

PREDICTABLY, Mick followed her into her bedroom. He pulled his shirt up over his head, revealing a chest so heartbreakingly perfect she wanted to weep. "I thought you said you were a pie purist?"

"I am." Sarah Jane set the berries and cream on the nightstand, then wiggled out of her clothes, leaving nothing but the apron on. "Who said the whipped cream was for pie?"

The look on Mick's face was priceless, and a slow, knowing smile slid over that endearingly sexy mouth. "You like shocking me, don't you? You like telling my heart that it's okay to have an attack."

"Wrong. I need you to stay healthy, otherwise I couldn't claim my consolation prizes."

He nodded, coming purposefully toward hers, his jeans unbuttoned and sagging at the waist, his manly feet bare. All male. All hers. "Ah, yes," he said. "And that would be a tragedy. I would hate for you to feel slighted."

Her gaze dropped to the impressive bulge in the front of his pants and a shuddering breath leaked out of her lungs. "I can assure you, I have yet to feel slighted." Her eyes widened considerably. "Overwhelmed, but never slighted."

Mick fingered the gauzy lace along the edge of her gingham apron. "Nice," he murmured.

"I'm glad you approve. Take off your pants."

He chuckled, much to her delight. "You're bossy."

"And yet it turns you on." She gave him a gentle shove onto the edge of her bed and quickly stripped his pants and boxers off, then swept them out of the way.

"Whatever gave you that idea?"

Sarah Jane painted the head of his penis with a mound of whipped cream, causing a hissing sound to emerge from between his teeth. She took him in her hand and deliberately licked it off. "This."

Mick lay back on the bed with a shaky laugh. "Oh, well. It's hard to argue with that evidence."

Sarah Jane grinned and licked him again, making a slow, deliberate path around the engorged head of his penis. "Or when the evidence is so hard...."

He let out a growl, one that moved into her bones. She suckled him deep, licked and laved, enjoying every inch of him. He was smooth and hard, slippery and wet, and she loved the way he felt against her tongue. Her body grew languid, yet energized with every pull of him deep into her throat. She cupped his tautened balls, gently playing with them as she upped the tempo, sucking harder, flicking her tongue over the sensitive head.

Mick's thigh muscles abruptly tightened, heralding his impending climax. As much as she wanted to keep tasting him, she wanted to feel him come inside of her more. She snatched a waiting condom from the bedside table, opened the package, then swiftly rolled it into place. A second later, she was straddling him. The first bump of him against her throbbing clit pushed the breath from her lungs, and feeling him slide inch by inch inside of her all but made her go boneless.

Mick leaned forward and latched on to a nipple, his hot mouth tugging at her, inadvertently pulling at a nerve that ran between her breast and her sex. She clamped her muscles around him, dragging up, then pushing back down, riding him—heaven help her, loving him—with her body… He was glorious beneath her, all sleek muscle and supple skin, with a dusting of hair over his chest.

Feeding at her breasts, pushing up inside of her…

The beginning of climax stirred in her achy womb and she rode him harder, her thighs burning from the exertion. Her breath came in winded little gasps, and with every thrust of his hips, she spiraled closer and closer to the point of no return. Mick bucked violently beneath her, moved to the other breast, suckling hard. It was down and dirty sex, Sarah Jane thought, knowing the time for tenderness would come later.

After they both did.

But right now she just wanted this—him, hot and hard, driving into her as though his very life depended on bringing her to release.

The orgasm caught her unaware, broadsided her. Her body contracted around him, every throbbing pulse weakening her further and further. Seconds later she was completely spent, wrung dry, but wet and satisfied.

Momentarily sated, Mick quickly rolled her onto her belly, dragged her hips up off the mattress and pushed into her from behind. "I. Love. Your. Ass," he said, punctuating each word with a hard thrust. He palmed her bottom lovingly, slid his hands over her rump in that possessive manner that put her in mind of a caveman. Or a beast. Or a hell-raiser.

Either way, she just knew she liked it.

He bent forward and licked the small of her back, making her arch into him, unwittingly meeting him. With every brutal push, his balls slapped at her aching flesh and, impossibly, she felt her sex ripen for release once again.

Too soon, she thought, certain she'd pass out from the pleasure.

He reached around and unerringly found her clit, making a vee with his fingers so that every thrust squeezed with just the right amount of pressure.

She shattered.

White turned to black and black to white, then the whole world went gray before returning to color. Sarah Jane's mouth opened in a scream, but she didn't hear it. Couldn't. Every sensation, every nerve ending, every bit of perception was concentrated between her legs, and it was all that she could do to cling to consciousness.

Mick thrust once, twice, three times, then buried himself to the hilt and stayed there. She could feel him pulsing inside of her, his big body quaking behind her, a pool of heat where his release gathered at the end of the condom.

He kissed the small of her back once more, carefully withdrew from her, removed the protection with the help of a tissue from the nightstand. Then, still breathing a bit unsteadily, he rolled her into the crook of his arm and tenderly stroked her hair.

"You know what I think, Sarah Jane?" he asked, his voice rusty and a bit weak.

She smiled against his chest, feeling safer and more content than she ever had in her life. "What, Mick?"

He pressed a reverent kiss to her temple. "I think you're the prize."

Her throat clogged with emotion. *And you've won me,* she thought, imagining handing her heart over to him, silently praying that he wouldn't break it.

14

"GRAMPS?"

A week later Mick drew up short at the sight of his grandfather coming out of the B and B.

"It's bad form to invite a man down for a visit, then stay out all night, boy," Charlie Chivers said. "I hope you're not getting into any trouble."

Only the kind that could ruin him, Mick thought, once again wondering what the hell he was doing with Sarah Jane.

Well, technically, he knew what he was doing—he was falling in love with her. Second by second, minute by minute, hour by hour, day by day he was growing more and more attached to her.

Unfortunately, his life was utterly directionless, and though he'd like nothing better than to stay in this cocoon of happiness he'd found with her for the past week, the more he thought about it, the guiltier he felt for dragging her into the fray. She was happy. She was content. She had a town she loved and a career she cared about.

Meanwhile, he was still at odds, without any sort of cohesive plan for his future. All he knew at the moment, besides the millions of little things he'd committed to memory about Sarah Jane, was that everything he touched eventually turned to shit, and he didn't want that to happen to her. He cared about her too much.

Though it had been a very unpleasant call—because he feared he'd be letting another friend down—he'd reached Huck on his cell phone this morning while Sarah Jane was in the shower, and let him know he wouldn't be returning to Atlanta or continuing to work for Ranger Security.

Huck had actually laughed. "I didn't figure you would, Mick. It's her, isn't it?"

Damn know-it-all, Mick thought. He'd never been able to get anything past his buddy. Levi, either, whom he'd also called. Past time, but better late than never.

Rather than answer Huck's leading question, he'd offered to reimburse the company for Chastity's lost income—thankfully, he had a sizable nest egg stashed away in savings—and could easily cover it.

Huck had assured him that wouldn't be necessary, then predictably asked him what his plans were.

Excellent question, Mick thought, still at a loss for any kind of an answer. Right now, other than finding that will for Sarah Jane and getting out of town before he could do any more harm, he didn't have one.

Coward, a little voice taunted. *You're scared. You're afraid of falling in love with her. You're afraid of letting her care for you. You're afraid of screwing this up, too.*

He wished he could argue with that little voice, tell it to go to hell, then eat blackberries from Sarah Jane's belly button for the rest of his life, but he knew better.

Until he got his head on straight, he didn't have any business getting closer to her, or worse yet, letting her get any closer to him. The idea of hurting her made his skin go clammy and his palms sweat.

And the idea of leaving her made him sick to his stomach.

But he couldn't do this. Not now. Not with her. Messing up his own life was one thing, wrecking hers was another. Hadn't he learned that with Carson Wells? Hadn't that nearly destroyed both of them?

This last week with Sarah Jane had been phenomenal. He'd gotten a glimpse of what his world could be like with her in it. Beer and pizza, hard work and a sense of satisfaction, laughter and love, hot sex and sweet affection. Apple-scented hair and blackberry tattoos, the click of puppy feet on a hardwood floor. Domestic. Wonderful. Happy. Things he'd never really contemplated before. He sighed.

But ultimately beyond his reach.

At least at the moment.

"What time did you get in, Gramps?" Mick asked as his grandfather began to stare at him with an odd expression. "I thought you said you couldn't make it."

"I changed my mind," he said. "I got into town about six last night, I reckon. Pretty little burg, isn't it? Hopping square. I played chess with a guy last evening, did a little flirting. Good food, too." He nodded. "That Mabel knows how to fry a chicken." His grandfather's faded blue eyes searched his. "How's the job coming?"

"It's not," Mick admitted, grimacing. In quick succession he presented the facts to Charlie, leaving out the bit about how he'd fallen for Sarah Jane, and concluding with his new and improved plan to beat the hell out of Cecil Simmons until he gave up the will. Naturally, he hadn't shared his alternate plan with Sarah Jane— she'd want to help, and he'd rather she stay out of it.

If anybody went to jail today, it would be him.

Charlie moved the toothpick he'd been chewing from one side of his mouth to the other, then said, "Sounds to me like this was a bad deal from the start, Micky. You never were a good liar. It's what made you such a good soldier."

Mick swallowed. "Thanks, Gramps."

"Of course, *I'd* be lying if I said I wasn't glad to see you out of the military. Too much action there for a guy like you. I knew you'd never settle down, find a wife and have a few babies so long as you were a Ranger."

Startled, Mick glanced up.

"Don't look so scared, boy," he said, chuckling under his breath. "Granted, loving a woman is a helluva lot more terrifying than war, but I'm sure you'll get the hang of it." He paused. "You need any help with that Simmons guy? I may be old, but I ain't dead yet. I've decided it's time to start living that way."

Pleased, Mick grinned. "Thanks, Gramps, but I'll handle it. I'd hate for you to miss any of the festival."

His grandfather clapped him on the back. "Don't you know it. I can't wait to get one of those blackberry fried pies you told me about. They're the talk of the town."

Whistling tunelessly, with a promise to see him later, Charlie made his way down the sidewalk and headed to the square. Sarah Jane, Mick knew, was already there, setting up and getting ready. He instinctively knew his grandfather would love her. She just had that way about her.

In fact, the best he could tell, the only people in town who didn't care for her were Chastity, who was jealous, and Cecil Simmons, who was screwing Chastity, so he disliked Sarah Jane by association.

It was time for both of them to leave his girl alone.

And good old Cecil was about to find that out the hard way.

Determined to catch the lawyer in his office before he, too, left for the festival, Mick quickly made his way to the man's place of business.

The receptionist looked up when he walked in. "Good morning. Can I help you?"

Mick grinned at her. "I sure hope so," he said, going into full-blown "aw-shucks" Southern-gentleman mode. "I don't have an appointment, but I could really use just a moment of Mr. Simmons's time. Would he happen to be available?"

She frowned. "I'm afraid he's finishing up a few things before he leaves to judge in the festival. Perhaps Monday would be better?"

Mick winced. "It really can't wait. I'll only take a minute." He aimed another smile at her, pleased when he saw her hesitate. "I promise," he added.

"All right." She relented. "Come with me." She knocked on Cecil's door. "Mr. Simmons, you've got a client here to see you. A Mr.—" She looked over her shoulder at him, waiting for him to fill in the blank.

"Chivers," Mick said.

"I thought you said I didn't have any appoint—"

Mick pushed through the door and carefully closed it before Cecil could get any further. He leveled a hard stare at the portly older man, taking note of the weak chin and receding hairline. He inwardly snorted. Definitely an easy mark for Chastity.

"Do you know who I am?" Mick asked.

There was a brief flicker of recognition before Cecil made the wrong choice and lied to him. "I'm afraid not," he said, smiling indulgently.

Mick walked forward, planted both fists on Cecil's desk and leaned in. "Then allow me to introduce myself. I'm Mick Chivers, former U.S. Army Ranger. I've been trained in lethal combat and can break your neck before you can blink." His voice hardened. "More importantly, I'm the man who's going to beat the hell out of you unless you produce George Walker's last will and testament. Am I making myself clear?"

The lawyer's gaze narrowed. "Is this a test? Did Chastity send you here?"

"I don't work for Chastity anymore, Mr. Simmons." Mick slammed his fist into the man's face, sending him reeling backward. Blood spurted from his nose—probably broken, Mick thought, tickled that he'd gotten to hit someone, because it actually made him feel better—and Cecil cried out in pain.

"Here's the way this is going to work," Mick explained. "You're going to get me that will so that I don't hit you again. And I'm going to promise not to have you disbarred for withholding it to start with."

The color leached from his face. "What? I—"

Mick came at him again.

"I'll get it!" Cecil screamed, cowering away.

"Mr. Simmons?" the receptionist called worriedly. "Are you okay?"

"Tell her you're fine," Mick said.

"I'm fine, Melissa," he answered in a nasal tone.

"Now get the will," Mick ordered.

With his handkerchief clutched to his face, Cecil ignored the filing cabinet and instead made his way to a bookcase on the far wall. He withdrew a leather-bound book—*The Count of Monte Cristo,* Mick realized, one of his favorite reads—and from within its pages, pulled a velum envelope.

Very reluctantly, Simmons handed it over.

Mick quickly withdrew the contents and, after a brief scan, once again met Cecil's gaze. His lips twisted bitterly. "Well, I can see why Chastity wasn't happy with this arrangement. She got a five thousand dollar settlement and the car, and Sarah Jane got everything else."

"She can fight it," Cecil said, drawing himself up.

"Oh? And who's going to represent that claim? You?" Mick grinned again. "I doubt it. But let me tell you what you are going to do. You are personally going to reimburse Sarah Jane every penny above five grand that Chastity has gone through."

Simmons's eyes widened in panic as he no doubt tallied up the plastic surgery, the new car, the deposit on the vacation home. "What? No! I can't possibly—"

"You can and you will, or I'll see to it that you're disbarred. The end. You don't have a choice, Cecil. You let Chastity take that away from you. Another protest and we'll tack on some emotional distress bucks for Sarah Jane. After all, you've put her through hell."

The older man seemed to deflate before his eyes. He had the most bewildered look. Lost, stupid and miserable. "I don't know what the hell I was thinking," he muttered.

Mick doubted whether he'd been thinking at all, but kept that tidbit to himself. With the will in hand, he walked to the door, then stopped short as another thought struck him. "One more thing. If her pie is the best, it wins. No taking this out on her."

Cecil drew himself up, as though his honor had been impugned. "Of course," he said. "I take my judging duties very seriously."

"Yeah, well, you'd have a lot more money right now if you'd given your lawyering duties the same attention." And with that parting shot, Mick left.

It was time to hand the will over, then do Sarah Jane an even bigger favor and get the hell out of her life while it was still on track. His chest ached at the very thought, and an odd pang pricked his conscience, but he straightened his spine and determinedly ignored both.

Man up, Chivers, he told himself. If it was easy, then it wouldn't be right, would it?

SARAH JANE DIDN'T KNOW what had happened between last night and early this morning, but somewhere in between, Mick had gotten…quiet.

And a quiet Mick, quite frankly, scared the hell out of her.

Her gaze slid to him now and, though she could tell he was happy that she'd won her fourth consecutive victory for her blackberry fried pies, she could also feel him pulling away. Retreating.

"Land sakes, girl, I think this is the best dessert I've

ever put in my mouth," Charlie Chivers, Mick's grand-father who'd arrived unexpectedly, told her. "I'll admit that peach used to be my favorite, but there's something in this that just makes it a little bit better." He took another bite and frowned thoughtfully. "You wouldn't tell me, now would you?"

Charmed, Sarah Jane grinned. "Sorry," she said. "It's a family secret."

He looked at his grandson, then glanced back at her, and a twinkle lit those familiar blue eyes. "I can wait," he said mysteriously. Sarah Jane frowned. What had he meant by that?

Mick sidled forward, his own eyes hidden behind his sunglasses. "Why do I feel like he's getting me in trouble?"

"I'm not getting you in trouble," Charlie said. He snorted. "You do enough of that on your own without any help."

"Thanks, Gramps," Mick told him. "Glad to know you've always got my back."

Merely chuckling, Charlie wandered over to Mabel's booth.

"Tina doesn't seem to be taking losing too hard," Mick said, jerking his head in her direction. Chase had arrived at their booth the minute the festival opened and, despite her protests, bought every single one of her pineapple cream cheese pies, determined that Mark Higgins—or any other man, for that matter—wasn't going to get another bite of Tina's cuisine.

Sarah Jane grinned, glad that Chase seemed to be coming around. "I'd say she's happier winning Chase back than a blue ribbon."

Mick inclined his head. He hesitated, and in that moment she could have sworn she heard her heart break. She knew what was coming. Instinctively knew that whatever he had to say was going to hurt her.

"Listen, Sarah Jane, I was wondering if we could go somewhere and talk for a moment."

Er…no. If she stayed here, she could keep it together. If she walked away with him, who knew what she would do? Make a fool of herself? Scream, cry, ask for another consolation prize?

She shook her head and pretended she didn't think anything was ominous about his request, when in reality she could already feel her legs shaking. "Actually, I shouldn't leave my booth."

"Oh."

"Is something wrong?"

He laughed darkly. "With you? No. With me? Everything." He looked away, smiled as he spotted his grandfather shamelessly flirting with Mabel. Mick released a breath, then withdrew a long envelope from his front pocket and handed it to her. His knuckles were scraped and bore the telltale signs of a recent fight. "I went to see Cecil this morning and I got this for you."

Sarah Jane's fingers went numb and her heartbeat kicked into an irregular rhythm. Her father's will? Stunned, her gaze flew to his. "Mick," she breathed.

"He's going to pay you back for every cent above what Chastity was supposed to get. Otherwise, I have promised to have him disbarred or worse." Mick gave a grunt of disgust. "It's no wonder she didn't want you to see it. I don't know if this was the will you saw, but in this one Chastity only gets five thousand dollars and your father's car. That's it."

Sarah Jane sank down onto her stool and carefully reviewed the paperwork. It was just as Mick had said. "No," she told him, swallowing hard. "This isn't the will I saw. Dad had left her his life insurance proceeds and part of his retirement fund…." She shook her head, flabbergasted. "He must have changed his mind, must have—" She stopped short as a handwritten note slipped from the pages. She instantly recognized her father's masculine scrawl, and a huge lump welled in her throat, making her gasp for breath.

You were always my first girl. I hope this proves it.
Love, Dad

That was it. Simple and to the point, a wealth of meaning behind a few little words. But that was her dad. Though she'd suspected that he'd realized he'd made a mistake, he was too proud to admit it to her face. Instead, generous as always, he'd done this instead.

Sarah Jane blinked back tears and looked up at Mick. "Thank you," she said, her voice clogged with unshed emotion. "I don't know how I'll ever make it up to you."

Mick swallowed, shifted awkwardly. "You don't have to. I just couldn't leave without making sure that you had it."

And there it was. She cleared her throat, inwardly bracing herself. She knew this about him. Knew that he was restless, and that ever trying to put a bridle on him would be an act of futility. She'd been telling herself that over and over from the moment she first saw him. "You're leaving?"

"Yeah," he said. He laughed, but the sound was brittle and completely unnatural. So unlike him. "I've, uh, I've got to get a résumé together, start looking for a job."

"I'm hiring," Sarah Jane said, laying it all on the line. She didn't so much as crack a smile. She was serious and he knew it.

Pain sliced across his woefully familiar face. "Sarah Jane, I—"

"You don't have to decide now, Mick," she said. "But you're a great carpenter and we work well together. Think about it," she added. "That's all I'm asking."

He seemed to be wrestling with a decision. His jaw worked and the ever-present shadow he never seemed able to shake darkened around him. "I have thought about it, Sarah Jane." He gave a bark of ironic laughter. "The thing is, everything I touch lately falls apart and I…I can't let that happen to you."

So he was saving her, was he? she wondered, instantly irritated. *Thank God,* Sarah Jane thought. Something she could get angry over. Of all the crack-brained, ridiculous, testosterone-inspired horseshit.

"Listen, Mick, while I appreciate the sentiment, I'm a big girl. I can look out for myself. If you want to bail on us—" she gestured between them "—on *this,* whatever's happening here, then at least pay me the courtesy of admitting that you're a coward or that you're just not interested. Don't tell me you're saving me, because that's total bullshit."

Though he didn't move a muscle, she felt a change in him. That perpetual tension reached breaking point.

"Bullshit, eh? How's this for bullshit? You want to know why I left the military, Sarah Jane? I'll tell you why. Because I made a bad call and sent a man over a ridge and almost got him killed, that's why." Mick's voice vibrated with self-loathing and pain, and her heart ached for him. "I almost cost a wife her husband and his children their father, because I ordered him to take a risk I should have taken. I went too far and he almost paid the price."

Sarah Jane felt herself soften. "Mick, you couldn't have known—"

He laughed darkly. "I know, and yet nobody seems to understand that it doesn't make a difference." He paused. "Another friend helped land me the placement with Ranger Security. First assignment, what do I do? I cross the line and get personally involved with you."

"Surely you don't think—"

"I know it was the right thing to do, Sarah Jane," Mick interrupted, passing a weary hand over his face. "But it doesn't change the fact that I have botched another job, and while I haven't ruined a friendship, I sure as hell haven't done it any favors. I feel like I've betrayed another trust."

Though she knew it was futile, she had to argue with him. Had to try and make him understand. "Mick, what you're describing is *life,* not bad luck or a losing streak. Life is messy, it's complicated. You get dirty. You get knocked down, then you pick yourself up again." She reached out and cupped his jaw. She lowered her voice. "These are setbacks, not a permanent way of life."

"Whatever my life is, Sarah Jane, it's a mess right now,

and it's not fair to drag you into it. I'm sorry." He exhaled heavily, then kissed her cheek, turned and walked away.

She watched him find his grandfather and tell him something, which made the older gentleman frown and look back at her. Charlie shook his head at her in apology and followed Mick away from the festivities.

Just her luck, Sarah Jane thought. She finally found a guy she could fall in love with, and the fool believed he was being noble by abandoning her. Tears burned her eyes and a lump the size of Arkansas swelled in her throat.

Tina wandered back into their booth. "Well, you were right," she announced happily. "Our evil plan worked. Chase has—" She drew up short, glimpsing Sarah Jane's face. "What's wrong?"

"You were right, too," she said. "S-sitting on *G*, w-waiting on *O*." She swallowed tightly. "He's gone."

Tina inhaled sharply. "Oh, honey," she said. "I'm so sorry."

Sarah Jane managed a watery smile and rattled the will significantly.

Her friend's eyes widened. "Is that what I think it is?"

"Yep." She snagged a napkin and blew her nose. "Come on," she said. "I'm going to console myself by evicting Chastity."

Then she'd work on evicting Mick from her heart.

15

One month later…

STILL A BIT IN SHOCK, Mick helped his grandfather load the last of his stuff onto the moving truck, then stepped back and closed the door. "I guess that's it, Gramps." He kicked at a loose pebble in the driveway. "Are you sure about this?"

"How many times have I got to answer that question?" Charlie grumbled. "I'm moving. I'm taking Morgan Freeman's advice from *Shawshank Redemption*. 'Member that line? 'Get busy living or get busy dying.'"

Mick swallowed a long-suffering sigh. Yes, he remembered. He'd only heard it about a dozen times over the past three weeks.

"Since I ain't ready to die, I reckon I'll live. I don't want to live here anymore, which I have explained to you repeatedly." Charlie paused and scratched his head. "Usually you ain't so thick. I don't know what your problem is. You've been in a terrible mood lately."

"I'm not thick," Mick explained, summoning

patience. "I just think you're making a snap decision based on Mabel's fried chicken and an annual festival centered around a dessert."

Honestly, when his grandfather had announced that he was moving to Monarch Grove—into Sarah Jane's old house, no less—Mick couldn't have been any more stunned than if Charlie had suddenly announced he was going to start buying foreign-made vehicles, or planned to march in a Gay Pride parade. Citing the need to be alone, Mick's grandfather—despite an interesting run-in with Byron, which had involved the breaking of glass and a few choice words about keeping his cold hands to himself—had stayed in Monarch Grove for a few days after his grandson had left. Mick had assumed it was to give him some space. He'd never dreamed the old man had actually been looking for a new place to live.

"Well, I hate moving off and leaving you, but you know where I am, and you're always welcome to visit," Charlie said. "That article in *Designing Weekly* has done amazing things for Sarah Jane's business, so I'm going to help her out until she finds a permanent partner," he added slyly, knowing it would drive Mick crazy. "That Sarah Jane," Charlie added fondly. "She's a pip. Hard worker, good heart, easy on the eyes." His grandfather stared at him. "A man could do a lot worse than a girl like her."

So he'd said, Mick thought, once again ignoring the pointed attempts at matchmaking. As if he didn't know exactly what kind of person Sarah Jane was. As if he didn't miss her with every fiber of his being, with every miserable beat of his heart.

Over the past month Mick had come within a gnat's ass of going back, of taking her up on her offer. After all, he sure as hell wasn't getting anything done here. He'd picked up breathing right where his grandfather had left off, maintaining the delicate balance of the Kentucky ecosystem. He inwardly snorted at the thought.

He'd been restless and miserable, like a cat pacing a cage, ever since he'd walked away from her. And no matter how many times he tried to tell himself that he was doing her a favor, that until he got his head screwed on straight he didn't need to become any more involved with her than he already was, Mick couldn't help but think he was a first-class full-of-shit ass.

His grandfather exhaled mightily, as though he'd finally lost patience with something. Or some*one*.

Namely him.

"Okay, Micky. I've got to say something to you." His bushy brows drew together in a straight line. "All my life, I've tried to make up for the fact that you pretty much got the shaft from your parents. I brought you home with me every summer and I taught you a trade, so that you'd always have a way to earn a living. No, I didn't make you a rocket scientist, but carpentry is honest work, and if it was good enough for Jesus, then I reckon it ought to be good enough for anybody." He paused. "But the one thing I haven't been able to teach you is something that you can't learn."

Mick blinked, confused. "If you can't teach it, then how can you learn it?"

"Don't sass me, boy," his grandfather snapped. His silver head bobbed with indignation. "It's good old common sense! Sorry to say so, but you don't seem to have any. Or you've lost it. Either way, you're making a total mess of things right now and, well, what sort of grandparent would I be if I didn't try to help?"

"The kind that doesn't insult and interfere?" he suggested.

"That's not my style."

He didn't think he'd be so lucky, Mick thought, swallowing a long-suffering sigh.

"Anyway, I know that you've been going through a rough patch lately. I can tell that your confidence is shot to hell, and with good reason. I'm not going to tell you not to blame yourself for that mistake with Carson Wells. But I would ask you to put one of those buddies you're so proud of into your shoes, and tell me if you thought they ought to feel responsible."

Mick paused. "You mean if it had been Huck or Levi who'd made the call to send Carson over the ridge?"

"That's exactly what I mean."

"I don't know," he said, though he was lying. Had it been one of them, he would have told them the same thing they'd been telling him for months. That they weren't mind readers and a soldier's orders were only as good as his intel.

"Well, I suggest you think on it," Charlie had told him. "And in the meantime, you need to get your butt back to Monarch Grove and patch things up with Sarah Jane."

"Gramps—"

"I saw the way you looked at her, Micky," his grandfather said, his voice low and knowing. "I may be old, but I'm not blind. You're in love with her."

It wasn't a question, but a statement, one that was accurate and on target.

"And you're miserable." Charlie slapped him on the arm. "Seems to me you need to follow Morgan Freeman's advice, too. Get busy living or get busy dying. Just because you're young doesn't mean you've got a golden ticket."

And with that parting advice, he clapped Mick on the back, climbed into the cab of the truck and drove away.

To Monarch Grove. To Sarah Jane.

An image of a big old home place, restored and filled with dark blond children and a menagerie of pets, the scent of blackberry pies in the oven, suddenly overwhelmed Mick. He imagined working with her every day, lying down with her every night, waking up with her every morning and all the wonderful things that could happen in between. Warm thighs, soft breasts, breakfast in bed, Christmas mornings...

He imagined his life with her, and knew every moment away from her was one wasted.

He'd been such an idiot, Mick thought, disgusted with himself. A total and complete idiot.

And stupidity of this order demanded a grand gesture. Thankfully, Sarah Jane had given him the information he needed to make one.

"Sarah Jane, I'm afraid I've got some bad news," Mason said, staring at her with a hangdog expression that instantly put her on alert.

In the process of putting her tools away, she stilled. They'd been working at another old house in a neighboring city for the better part of two weeks, and had finally finished the salvage. Deciding a vacation was in order after such a hard summer—not to mention the whole broken-heart thing—she'd booked a condo in Orange Beach, and was looking forward to taking a bagful of books and some sunscreen, and hitting the sand for a little relaxation. If Mason's bad news jeopardized her plans, she'd quite possibly pitch a good old-fashioned, bucket-kicking fit, turning her inner redneck loose.

"What?" she asked cautiously.

"That was Carl," he said, gesturing to his cell phone. "Imogene Childress has sold Ponder Hill."

Horrified, Sarah Jane gasped. Shock lanced through her. "But I just tried to buy it from her a couple of weeks ago! She swore she wasn't going to sell!" Sarah Jane began to pace, shoving her hands into her hair, pulling until her scalp ached. "Did he say who bought it?"

Maybe if she offered that person enough money, she could convince them to sell. She felt tears prick the back of her eyes, and resisted the urge to drop onto her rear end and squall. Honestly, she hadn't shed a tear over Mick—she'd told herself that crying indicated she'd given up on him, and she hadn't—but losing that house, her dream home, suddenly made everything else, every repressed emotion, every bit of irritation, fear, longing and hope, bubble up within her and pour out of her eyes.

Huge sobs caught in her throat, then escaped, one gasp at a time.

Seemingly unsure of what to do, Mason hurried over and put a scrawny arm around her shoulders. "Oh, Sarah Jane, don't cry. Carl says the buyer is interested in restoring the house and won't work with anyone but you. I told him we'd go straight out there."

Sarah Jane hiccupped and looked up. "What? Restore the house?"

"Yes," Mason said. "That's good news, right?"

"No, Mason," she said, even more miserable. Now, not only was she not going to live in her dream house, she was going to be asked to restore it to someone else's specs. She shook her head. Nope. She couldn't do it. "Call Carl back and tell him the buyer is going to have to come up with an alternate solution. I'm not doing it."

Mason blinked, seemingly certain he'd misunderstood. And with good reason—she'd never turned down work before. But this was one job she couldn't do.

"Sarah Jane, at least meet with the guy. See what his plans are."

She frowned. "It's a guy?"

He nodded. "That was my understanding. It's on the way home. Let's just swing by and see what he has to say."

She'd swing by and kiss her dreams goodbye, Sarah Jane thought. Make a final wish on her angel. But she'd be damned if she'd fix up her house for someone else.

Twenty minutes later, she climbed out of the truck and stared up at the old mansion, her throat tight. Rather than join her, Mason powered the window down. "I'm going to run down to Carl's for a minute. He asked me to come by and check his computer. He's having some trouble."

Sarah Jane frowned. He was leaving? "Mason—"

"Go on inside," he said, making shooing motions. "I'll be right back." And with that odd behavior, he was off.

Oh, well, she thought. It didn't look as if the new

owner was here, either, which was actually kind of nice. She'd like to spend a minute in the old house before she left, to say goodbye. She doubted whoever it was would appreciate her habit of breaking and entering. Then again, she'd been in jail before and had survived the experience.

She lingered a minute in every room, once again imagining how she would have restored things, arranged the furniture, put up her Christmas tree and installed her claw-foot tub. Ridiculous, she knew, but she couldn't help it. She'd always, always loved this house.

Eventually she made her way upstairs, to her favorite spot in the whole place, her angel window overlooking the property. Another lump welled in her throat as she stared out across the landscape.

She had one wish left, Sarah Jane thought. She'd better make it count. "Send him back to me," she whispered, tracing the angel's robe with her index finger. "Please."

Mick stepped out from a bedroom on the right, startling her. She inhaled sharply and clasped a hand over her mouth. That gorgeous smile, sexy and irreverent and just the slightest bit unsure, curled his lips. "Hi, Sarah Jane."

She stared at him, unable to make it all make sense. "You?" she asked, her voice raw with emotion. "You bought this house?"

He nodded. "I did. It took a bit of persuading and more cash than I'd planned to part with, but after everything I've put you through…I thought it would make a nice—" his gaze tangled with hers "—consolation prize."

She blinked, confused. Consolation prize? Everything he'd put her through?

"It's yours, Sarah Jane," he said patiently. "I bought it for you. Actually, I bought it for us, but I didn't want to get ahead of myself." Again that endearing smile appeared, the one that made her heart ache.

God, she'd missed him.

She cleared her throat again. "Considering you bought the house before talking to me, I'd say you've already done that."

"I wanted to make a grand gesture," he said. "See if I could get rid of that Squatting Snake in the Grass moniker. Maybe exchange it for something a little better. Like Warrior Bleeding Heart's Husband?"

Sarah Jane grew utterly still as the impact of that little question rocketed through her. "Husband?"

He shrugged. "I'm already doing everything else backward. Thought I might as well go for broke and throw a proposal in there," he explained, as though this logic was completely reasonable.

"For the record, Mick, typically, women like it when a man gets down on one knee and offers a ring."

He sidled closer and slid the pad of his thumb over her bottom lip. "Maybe so, but I'm not asking a typical woman. I'm asking you." His voice grew raspy, as though his throat was closing up, and his brilliant blue eyes pierced her. "And you are anything but ordinary, Sarah Jane."

He couldn't have found a compliment she would have appreciated more, she realized, her chest so full she feared it would burst. "Do you want an answer now?" she asked, wrapping her arms around his neck.

Mick dropped his forehead against hers in relief. "Now would be nice, yes."

She tsked regretfully. "My life is a mess right now. I don't know if it would be fair to drag you into it," she said, shooting his words right back at him.

He laughed, the wretch, then lifted her off her feet and planted a long, hot kiss on her lips. Her insides melted. "Life's messy, Sarah Jane. But I'd rather be in a mess with you than anywhere else."

She grinned, realizing that every wish she'd ever made to her angel had come true in this moment. She rocked suggestively against him. "Then let's get dirty."

Epilogue

One Year Later…

"Well, what do you think?" Mick asked.

Sarah Jane surveyed the outside of the house with a critical eye. "That wreath," she said, pointing. "It needs to be a hair to the right."

He expelled an exasperated breath, but did his wife's bidding. "Isn't that the one I just moved a hair to the left?"

"Yes, but I was wrong then." She beamed at him as he made the correction. "Yep, that's better."

"I'm glad," he said, climbing down off the ladder. "I prefer the name Ponder Hill to The Widow-maker. And if I have to adjust another damned Christmas wreath I'm going to—"

She stopped his words with a long, slow kiss. "Take me inside and make love to me before a roaring fire?" she suggested silkily.

Mick growled low in his throat and smiled down at her. "That sounds like an excellent plan." He looked through the parlor-room window and sighed. "I'm assuming you mean after our guests leave?"

She squeezed his waist. "We have four fireplaces," she offered. "Surely one of those would work. I'm partial to the one in the upstairs bathroom."

Ah, a wonderful idea, he decided. Happier than he could ever imagine himself being, Mick felt a contented grin slide over his lips. "Have I ever mentioned that I like the way you think?"

"Maybe once or twice." She kissed the underside of his jaw, slid her hand up his chest and into the hair at his nape.

"How long until we can run them off?" Mick asked.

"Let's let them watch it one more time, then send them packing."

The "it" in question being their most recent ultra-sound DVD. Charlie and Mabel, as well as Tina and Chase—who'd moved into Sarah Jane's old family home the instant she'd evicted Chastity—were all looking forward to welcoming the next generation of potential pranksters. Mick grinned. True to form, they were beginning their family in proper hell-raising, she-devil style—with twins, a boy and girl.

Now *that* was a compensation prize.

And he had one more for his lovely wife. Mick withdrew a little box from his pocket and handed it to her. "An early Christmas present," he explained at her uncertain look. Funny how the holidays used to be the most miserable time of the year for him, but now he looked forward to them with all the zeal of a kid who still believed in Santa Claus.

Smiling, Sarah Jane removed her gloves and care-fully opened the box. She frowned at the little piece of paper she found inside. "What's this?"

"Look at it," Mick said.

She flipped it over and back, studying both sides, a questioning expression on her face. "It looks like an old receipt."

"It is," he confirmed. "For the stained glass window upstairs. Look at the name on the receipt."

A second later, her delighted gasp echoed between them, warming his heart. "Lillian Mae Walker. But that's—"

"Your great-great-grandmother," he stated. "You were right about your connection to the house. Lillian made your wishing angel."

Sarah Jane's eyes sparkled with tears of joy. "How did you find this?" she asked.

He shrugged. "Imogene kept good records, and made it a point to keep everything that had to do with this house. It was just a matter of going through her old files."

Sarah Jane's gaze dropped back down to the receipt, then to the upstairs window, after which she hugged him tightly. "Have I mentioned that I love you?" she asked.

"You have," Mick said. "Have I mentioned that I love *you?*"

She pressed a kiss to his jaw. "All the time, and in ways I never expect."

He grinned. "Good. I'm The Hell-raiser, you know. I'd hate to be predictable."

She chuckled softly. "Impossible," she said. "Utterly impossible."

* * * * *

He cautioned himself to be leery. He was human and he'd been conned before. But never by anyone nearly so attractive. Never by anyone he'd felt so attracted to.

In her defense, Nick supposed that Georgie could actually be telling him the truth. That she was a victim in all this. He had his people back in California checking her out, to make sure she was who she said she was and had, as she claimed, not even been near a computer but on the road these last few months that the threats had been made.

In the meantime, he was doing his own checking out. Up close and exceedingly personal. So personal he could feel his blood stirring.

It had been a long time since he'd thought of himself as anything other than a law enforcement agent of one type or other. But Georgeann Grady made him remember that beneath the oaths he had taken and his devotion to duty, there beat the heart of a man.

A man who'd been far too long without the touch of a woman.

He watched as the light from the fireplace caressed

the outline of Georgie's small, trim, jean-clad body as she moved about the rustic living room that could have easily come off the set of a Hollywood Western. Except that it was genuine.

As genuine as she claimed to be?

Something inside of him hoped so.

He wasn't supposed to be taking sides. His only interest in being here was to guarantee Senator Joe Colton's safety as the latter continued to make his bid for the presidency. Everything else was supposed to be secondary, but, Nick had to silently admit, that was just a wee bit hard to remember right now.

Earlier, before she'd put her precocious handful of a daughter to bed, Georgie had fed his appetite by whipping up some kind of a delicious concoction out of the vegetables she'd pulled from her garden. Vegetables that, by all rights, should have been withered and dried. She'd mentioned that a friend came by on occasion to weed and tend it. Still, it surprised him that somehow she'd managed to make something mouthwatering out of it.

Almost as mouthwatering as she looked to him right at this moment.

Again, he was reminded of the appetite that hadn't been fed, hadn't been satisfied.

And wasn't going to be, Nick sternly told himself. At least not now. Maybe later, when things took on a more definite shape and all the questions in his head were answered to his satisfaction, there would be time to explore this feeling. This woman. But not now.

Damn it.

"Sorry about the lack of light," Georgie said,

breaking into his train of thought as she turned around to face him. If she noticed the way he was looking at her, she gave no indication. "But I don't see a point in paying for electricity if I'm not going to be here. Besides, Emmie really enjoys camping out. She likes roughing it."

"And you?" Nick asked, moving closer to her, so close that a whisper would have trouble fitting in. "What do you like?"

The very breath stopped in Georgie's throat as she looked up at him.

"I think you've got a fair shot of guessing that one," she told him softly.

* * * * *

Be sure to look for COLTON'S SECRET SERVICE and the other following titles from **THE COLTONS: FAMILY FIRST** *miniseries:*
RANCHER'S REDEMPTION by Beth Cornelison
THE SHERIFF'S AMNESIAC BRIDE
by Linda Conrad
SOLDIER'S SECRET CHILD by Caridad Piñeiro
BABY'S WATCH by Justine Davis
A HERO OF HER OWN by Carla Cassidy

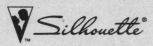

Romantic
SUSPENSE

Sparked by Danger,
Fueled by Passion.

The Coltons Are Back!

Marie Ferrarella
Colton's Secret Service

The Coltons: Family First

On a mission to protect a senator, Secret Service agent
Nick Sheffield tracks down a threatening message only
to discover Georgie Gradie Colton, a rodeo-riding single
mom, who insists on her innocence. Nick is instantly
taken with the feisty redhead, but vows not to let his
feelings interfere with his mission. Now he must figure
out if this woman is conning him or if he can trust her
and the passion they share....

Available September wherever books are sold.

Look for upcoming Colton titles
from Silhouette Romantic Suspense:

Visit Silhouette Books at www.eHarlequin.com   SRS27598

REQUEST YOUR FREE BOOKS!

2 FREE NOVELS
PLUS 2
FREE GIFTS!

HARLEQUIN®

Blaze™
Red-hot reads!

SPECIAL EDITION™

NEW YORK TIMES BESTSELLING AUTHOR

DIANA PALMER

A brand-new Long, Tall Texans novel

HEART OF STONE

Feeling unwanted and unloved, Keely returns to Jacobsville and to Boone Sinclair, a rancher troubled by his own past. Boone has always seemed reserved, but now Keely discovers a sensuality with him that quickly turns to love. Can they each see past their own scars to let love in?

Available September 2008
wherever you buy books.

HARLEQUIN®
Blaze™

COMING NEXT MONTH

#417 ALL OR NOTHING Debbi Rawlins
Posing undercover as a Hollywood producer to investigate thefts at the
St. Martine hotel has good ol' Texas cowboy Chase Culver sweatin' under
his Stetson. All the up-close contact with the hotel's gorgeous personal trainer
Dana McGuire isn't helping either, and she's his prime suspect!

#418 RISQUÉ BUSINESS Tawny Weber
Blush
Delaney Connor can't believe the way her life has changed! The former mousy
college professor is now a TV celebrity, thanks to a makeover and a talent for
reviewing pop fiction. She's at the top of her game—until bad boy author
Nick Angel tests her skills both as a reviewer…and as a woman.

#419 AT HER PLEASURE Cindi Myers
Who knew science could be so…sensual? For researcher Ian Marshall his
summer of solitude on an uninhabited desert island becomes much more
interesting with the arrival of Nicole Howard. And when she offers a no-
strings-attached affair, how can he resist?

#420 SEX & THE SINGLE SEAL Jamie Sobrato
Forbidden Fantasies
When something feels this taboo, it has to be right. That's how Lieutenant
Commander Kyle Thomas explains her against-the-rules lust for her
subordinate Drew MacLeod. So when she finally gets the chance to seduce
him, nothing will stand in her way.

#421 LIVE AND YEARN Kelley St. John
The Sexth Sense, Bk. 6
When Charles Roussel runs into former flame Nanette Vicknair, he knows
she's still mad at his betrayal years ago. But before he can explain, he's cast
adrift in a nether world, neither alive nor dead. Except, that is, in her bed every
night. There he proves to her that he's truly the man of her dreams!

#422 OVERNIGHT SENSATION Karen Foley
Actress Ivy James has just hit the big time. She's earned the lead role in a
blockbuster movie based on the true-to-life sexual experiences of war hero
Garrett Stokes, and her costar is one of Hollywood's biggest and brightest
actors. The problem? The only one she wants to share a bed with—on-screen
and off—is Garrett himself!

HBCNM0808

www.eHarlequin.com